# Her
# Noble
# Groom

## C.V. Lee

Her Noble Groom

Library of Congress Cataloging-in-Publication Data is available upon request.

Library of Congress Control Number: 2025913627

ISBN:  979-8-9870319-4-0 (paperback)

ISBN:  979-8-9870319-5-7 (eBook)

Cover Design by: GetCovers.com

# CONTENTS

*To my husband, John*

*The man who is my own personal James. This year, we celebrated our thirty-sixth wedding anniversary. Words can never express my gratitude that God sent you into my life. You brought music back into my heart and put a song on my lips.*

*Thank you for supporting me through all my harebrained schemes, including my journey to becoming a writer and an author. You always believed in me and loved me. You are my knight in shining armor—albeit without the armor, the sword, or the horse.*

# PREFACE

Dear Reader,

I am delighted to bring you the story of Thomasse and James. They are fictional characters from my novels Token of Betrayal and Betrayal of Trust. I love these secondary characters and wanted to share their love story. This novella can be read as a standalone, there is no need to read the aforementioned novels to appreciate their story. After, please read the Author's Notes for additional background.

I would love to hear your thoughts on these characters and their story. You can share your feedback by leaving a review on Goodreads, or Amazon. Or reach out to me directly at c.v.lee.writer@gmail.com.

This story explores difficult themes. If you prefer content warnings, they are on the following page. Happy reading!

*C.V. Lee*

# CONTENT WARNING

My goal in writing this book is to offer a message of hope to those who have endured trauma. Difficult topics such as grief, sexual assault, and suicidal ideation are explored. No acts of violence occur on the page—rather they are alluded to or discussed in separate settings. My intention is to provide comfort rather than distress.

On my own journey, I found solace in knowing I was not alone. We all have our own path to healing, each is different, each in our own time, and some may carry it forever. But we all deserve love and the chance to live our best lives.

If you or someone you know is struggling, please seek support. You are not alone.

# GLOSSARY

## Clothing

- Coif – hood-shaped cap, or skullcap, with extended sides, can also be made of chain mail

- Cotehardie – a close-fitting outer garment with long sleeves, laced or buttoned down the front or back

- Girdle – belt or band worn around the waist

- Hauberk – chain mail shirt

- Hose – close-fitting legwear; originally two separate pieces, joined into one garment with a codpiece by the late 15$^{th}$ century

- Kirtle – a loose garment; worn under a gown by upper-class women or often as an outer garment by lower-class women

- Tunic – a simple, T-shaped garment, usually belted, worn over a linen shirt or chemise, varying in length based on gender and class

- Patten – protective overshoe, usually wooden, worn to elevate the feet and protect from the mud and filth

## Other Terms

- Cette garce – this bitch (archaic/slang, now vulgar)

- Costrel – flask made of leather, earthenware, or wood, with an ear so it can be suspended from the waist, like a canteen

- Cumberground – useless person who just takes up space

- Demoiselle – title for a noblewoman, often unmarried, but used for married women on Jersey during the 15th century

- Leech – archaic for physician

- Manor – a self-sufficient estate over which the seigneur had authority and governance

- Mumble crust – toothless beggar or muttering fool

- Palfrey – riding horse suitable for a woman

- Seigneur – French term for feudal lord used on the Channel Islands

- Tussie-mussie – small bunch of flowers

# PRONUNCIATION GUIDE

Like others, I find it frustrating to read a book when I cannot figure out how to say some of the names. Below is a list of the most difficult terms to pronounce:

- St. Ouen sounds like "saint wahn"

- Orgueil sounds like "or guy"

- Thomasse sounds like either "tom mas see" or "tom ma say." Either is correct.

# *MAP*

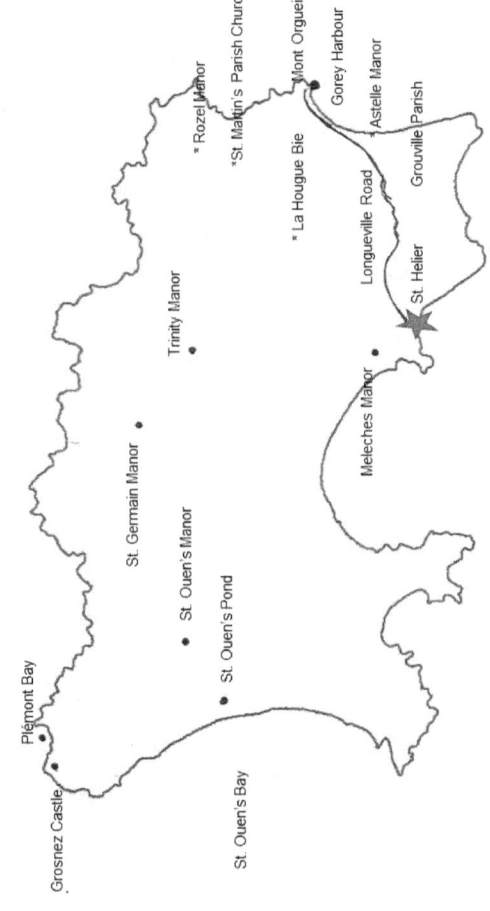

Isle of Jersey

- Grosnez Castle
- Plémont Bay
- St. Ouen's Bay
- St. Ouen's Pond
- St. Ouen's Manor
- St. Germain Manor
- Trinity Manor
- " Rozel Manor
- "St. Martin's Parish Church
- Mont Orgueil
- Gorey Harbour
- Astelle Manor
- Grouville Parish
- " La Hougue Bie
- Longueville Road
- St. Helier
- Meleches Manor

## Chapter One

Sussex, England. February 23, 1461

Thomasse twirled before the looking glass, the dark green velvet skirt of her gown swirling about her ankles. Embroidered silver leaves adorned the trumpet sleeves and hem, and the matching silver girdle accentuated her tiny waist. Tonight, she would step into her mother's role as the manor's hostess, hoping to catch the eye of a certain gentleman, and prove herself a desirable match. "Sir Arthur cannot fail to notice me tonight."

The maidservant furrowed her brow as she adjusted the folds of the skirt. "Not so long ago, it was Robert. And Harold before him. There have been so many, I have lost count."

Thomasse tossed her head. "I was a young girl then. Now, I am of marrying age and must be more discerning in my choice of beaus."

"Turning sixteen does not, by some miracle, endow a maiden with great wisdom," the maidservant replied. "Pray, what makes Sir Arthur worthy of your regard?"

"Agnes!" Thomasse gasped. "Surely, you jest." She raised a finger. "First, he is handsome." She raised another finger. "Second, he owns a large estate in Berkshire." She raised a third finger. "And he is highly favored by the king. What more could a maiden desire?"

Agnes struggled to her feet. "All those can be lost in the twinkling of an eye. But a man who listens, who is gentle and kind—he is the one worth cleaving to."

Pushing her feet into a pair of brocade slippers, Thomasse laughed. "Sounds horribly dull!"

Agnes flinched ever so slightly, and Thomasse regretted her thoughtless words, but only for a fleeting moment before her mind returned to the festivities already underway below. With Lent beginning on the morrow, this would be the last party for some time.

Agnes limped to the dressing table and fetched the bottle of jasmine oil. Thomasse dabbed a bit on her wrists and behind her ears, then drew a long, blonde curl over her shoulder. *Perfection!*

"My late husband—"

"Another time, Agnes. My guests await."

Thomasse glided out the door and into the passageway overlooking the great hall below. Torches flickered, their flames casting shadows that danced across the ceiling, giving the room an air of enchantment, the perfect setting to spark romance.

The sweet strains of a lute mingled with the steady buzz of conversation and the crackle of the fire on the hearth. White-clothed tables lined the walls, leaving the center open for the night's amusements.

She leaned against the rail and surveyed the room. The ladies' colorful gowns were a blessed relief from the gray of winter. A burst of laughter caught her attention. A group of gentlemen, including Arthur, was congregated in the middle of the room, deep in conversation.

Warmth suffused her body as she observed her beloved. Arthur's murrey tunic complemented the dark auburn of his hair, while the pale-colored hose revealed the length and strength of his legs. The tilt of his chin and the confidence of his stance were alluring. How would he respond if she eased in beside him and slipped her hand into his?

She willed him to look her direction, but his gaze drifted toward the stairs where her friends Lady Eleanor and Lady Maud waited. Eleanor dipped her golden head, a hint of a smile playing on her lips. Thomasse placed a hand on her stomach, trying to quell the sudden queasiness that arose. Surely Arthur had not been seeking out Eleanor. Her smile had been politeness, nothing more.

Thomasse hastened the length of the passage and descended the stairs, smiling brightly. But Arthur had already reverted his attention to his friends. Her smile faded and her spirit flagged, but only for a moment. The night was young. There would be ample opportunity to weave her charms.

She lifted her chin, shoving aside her doubts, and joined her friends. Together, they evoked the beauty of a summer garden—Eleanor, a vision in rose-colored silk, Maud in bright yellow, and she in green.

Thomasse addressed Eleanor. "I hope your journey here was without incident."

"Other than the rain, there is little to report," Eleanor replied, although the brightness of her eyes and the flush of her cheeks hinted at something more than just exposure to the elements, and Thomasse resolved to discover Eleanor's secret before the evening was through.

Eleanor touched Thomasse's sleeve, outlining the leaves with her fingertip. "Your gown is magnificent."

"Do you think it will be sufficient to catch Sir Arthur's eye?" Thomasse whispered in Eleanor's ear.

Eleanor's gaze shifted to Arthur. "I dare not say lest I give you false hope and you blame me." She shivered. "I am still quite chilled from the ride."

"Let us move nearer the hearth," Maud said, grasping Eleanor's and Thomasse's hands, leading the way.

As they wove through the crowd of guests, Thomasse caught snippets of conversations—"rumblings in the north," "Edward of York," and "Warwick." When they neared the group of young men, their conversation ceased.

"I am pleased you could join us this evening." Although Thomasse addressed the group, her gaze lingered on Arthur. "I hope the party meets with your approval."

"Indeed," Arthur replied, bestowing Thomasse with a heart-stopping smile, but his gaze quickly strayed. "Lady Eleanor, 'tis a pleasure to see you again."

Eleanor flushed. This was the second time within minutes that Arthur's and Eleanor's gaze had met, hinting at a familiarity that had not previously existed. It puzzled Thomasse. She and Arthur had been friends from their youth, yet his behavior suggested they were mere acquaintances. Did he not recall those summer days when they played together by the creek, catching frogs and skipping stones? Or the time he gallantly rescued her from the tree when the hem of her skirt caught on a branch?

Maud tugged their hands, and they moved closer to the hearth.

Eleanor stretched her hands to the warmth. "Lady Maud, have you any fresh gossip?"

Maud fidgeted with the rosary hanging from her brown leather girdle. "Maybe it is too soon to reveal—"

"Then you must tell," Eleanor said, "for we are your dearest friends."

Maud gestured for them to lean in close. "I have been chosen as one of Queen Margaret's ladies-in-waiting."

Eleanor clapped her hands. "Such marvelous news. No one deserves it more than you. Oh, the stories you shall tell!"

Thomasse clasped Maud's hand. "I hope this does not affect you joining us on our trip to the Continent."

"I cannot say," Maud replied. "I hope the queen can spare me."

Distracted by Arthur's nearness, Thomasse cast furtive glances his way, hoping to catch his eye. A lull in Maud and Eleanor's chatter drew her attention back just as a manservant approached.

He bowed. "Mistress Thomasse, Master Nicholas requests your presence in the study."

Thomasse pressed her lips together. "Can it not wait?"

"He commanded me summon you forthwith," he replied, then retreated into the crowd.

Thomasse made a slight curtsey to her friends. "Excuse me. I shall return shortly."

She wended her way across the great hall, stopping often to greet guests. Reaching the other side, she turned into the short passage which led to the study. Her father was bent over his desk writing, a single beeswax candle lit the parchment, leaving most of the room in shadow.

"Father," she said, hesitantly. "You asked for me?"

He set the quill aside and pushed his graying shoulder-length hair behind his ear. "Yes, Mistress Thomasse. I want you to meet Lord John Courtenay."

A tall man emerged from the shadows. The candle's light reflected in the round ruby pinned to his roll-brimmed hat. A gloved hand rested on the pommel of his jeweled sword, and the fine cut of his red and yellow bi-colored tunic bespoke his loyalty to King Henry and the House of Lancaster. She judged him to be in his mid-twenties.

4

"Lord Jack is Lady Eleanor's brother."

Thomasse curtsied. "Pleased to make your acquaintance. How odd Lady Eleanor has never spoken of you."

"She has seen little of me," Jack replied. "I entered the service of the Percy household when Lady Eleanor was still young. I have only recently returned to Devon."

"Lord Jack is involved in the tin mining trade," her father said.

Jack cocked his head. "The disadvantage of being the second son of an earl—I inherited neither estate nor title. Still, I have made the most of my misfortune. My endeavors earn me a good income and the means to purchase a large property with a comfortable home."

"Your father would be proud." Thomasse looked from one to the other, unsure how their conversation involved her.

Her father rose and came to stand beside her. "My daughter has been taught to read and write. She also speaks fluent French and sings like a nightingale."

"Impressive." Jack studied her, pondering each detail. "She is as handsome as you promised. I consider myself most fortunate."

"Excellent," her father replied, shaking Jack's hand. "My solicitor will draw up the terms. We can finalize the details after Easter."

Thomasse's eyes widened. "You cannot mean—"

Her father's eyes gleamed. "Yes, you are to be wed. Once the contract is signed, it will seal your espousal to Lord Jack, a union which will bring great advantage to both our families."

Her voice trembled as she spoke. "Should I not have been consulted?"

Jack's body stiffened, and his hand gripped his sword.

Her father glared his disapproval. "Please excuse my daughter's outburst. Give us a moment."

Jack bowed and strode from the room; the door clicked shut behind him.

Her father scowled. "Such insolent behavior is unpardonable. Lord Jack is an honorable man and soon to be your husband."

"If you had told me about this afore—"

"My apologies. I thought I had."

"Well, you did not." She pointed at the door. "How can you expect me to marry someone I have just met?"

Her father waved his hand in dismissal. "You have your whole life to get to know him. With your dowry and his connections, you will be respected and live in comfort."

"But you promised mother I could marry whom I pleased."

"That is unfair. Your mother was dying," her father replied. "I would have promised her anything to relieve her anguish."

Thomasse clenched her teeth. "You cannot force me to marry him. Besides, my heart belongs to another."

"Saith the maiden who giveth her heart on a whim."

"My regard is steadfast."

He took her hands in his. "How many men have engaged your affections this past year? And your current flame does not return your regard."

Thomasse's cheeks burned, and she could not meet her father's eyes. "What do you know of my beloved's sentiments?"

"Do you imagine I have not noticed how you pine after him? Truly, I pity you being enamored with your friend's betrothed."

Her breath caught. "Of whom do you speak?"

"Of Lady Eleanor and Sir Arthur. Surely you know of their betrothal." Her father returned to his chair behind the desk. "That is why I thought a marriage to Lord Jack would please you. You and Lady Eleanor will be sisters."

Thomasse dropped into the chair opposite. "So you thought to condemn me to a life of misery, forced to see him wed to my dearest friend?" She lifted a hand to her brow. "Such a cruel twist of fate. How am I to bear it?"

Her father shook his head. "It is time to lay aside your youthful fancies. You shall wed before Pentecost. Under Lord Jack's protection, I know you will be safe."

Thomasse refused to look at her father. Her whole life had been upended ere she could draw a breath, because two men agreed to something in their own interests without regard for her wishes. The idea was intolerable.

She leaned forward, placing her elbows on the desk. "What of your promise to take my friends and me on tour to the Continent? You would not go back on your word."

He picked up the quill. "Circumstances change. They will soon forget."

Thomasse sprang from the chair, unable to abide her father's presence any longer, and hastened from the room,

"You owe Lord Jack an apology," he called after her. "Sooner is better."

Not ready to apologize or return to the festivities, she stole away to a darkened corner. A tear slid down her cheek. Was she so daft that she had not noticed a growing regard between Eleanor and Arthur? After what she witnessed this evening, she could not deny the attraction. How humiliating! To think she had poured out her deepest secret to her best friend, yet Eleanor had never deigned to disclose the truth.

She dashed a hand across her cheek, wiping away the wetness. If only she could flee to her chamber; but as hostess, she must put on a brave face for their guests. She straightened her shoulders and glided into the great hall, a smile painted on her face.

Much as her mind and body resisted, she knew she must seek out Jack first. She found him at the sideboard, pouring himself a tankard of ale. "Lord Jack, allow me to apologize. The news was unexpected."

Jack finished pouring the ale and took a long draught. "Accepted. I imagine my reaction might be similar given the circumstances."

"You are most kind."

Thomasse took her leave and rejoined her friends. With so many thoughts jangling inside her head, she scarcely heard a word Eleanor and Maud said. No wonder Eleanor had preened like a courtly maiden. She had known secrets she must withhold.

"Mistress Thomasse." Maud's voice invaded her thoughts. "You seem troubled. What did your father say?"

"Not here. Not now," Thomasse hissed.

Eleanor grabbed her hand, and Maud followed as Eleanor led Thomasse to a quiet corner.

"Do not keep us waiting," Eleanor said. "Lady Maud has already shared her good tidings."

7

Thomasse took a deep breath, not wanting to sound peevish, although she felt it. She glared at Eleanor. "Why did you not tell me?"

"What is she talking about?" Maud asked.

"I speak of her betrothal to Sir Arthur," Thomasse replied.

Maud gasped. "Is it really true?"

Eleanor flushed. "I thought it wrong to share such news by letter. I wanted to tell you both in person, but I did not get the chance." She turned to Thomasse. "I hope you are happy we shall be sisters."

"Sisters?" Maud whispered loudly.

"Yes, my father just informed me of my own impending betrothal to Lady Eleanor's brother," Thomasse replied. "Someone who I have only met tonight and know nothing of his past."

"I assure you, my brother is an honorable man," Eleanor said excitedly. "Just think, we both are to be married soon."

The trumpet blared, calling the guests to supper. Thomasse was grateful to be seated on the dais, even if it was beside her father, relieved to be separated from her friends. There was no need to make a pretense that nothing was amiss.

The guests flocked to the tables. Gluttony and drunkenness would rule the evening, for on the morrow, forty days of privation would begin. When all were seated, menservants filed in, their arms laden with platters of roasted meats, cheeses, fruit, bread, and nuts. Butlers poured wine into silver chalices for the esteemed guests while the common folks were given tankards of ale.

Although the cooks had prepared her favorite dishes, Thomasse had little appetite. Unable to keep her mind engaged on the surrounding conversation, she tried to take pleasure in the night's entertainment: jugglers, mummers, and minstrels playing their instruments, regaling the guests with songs, stories, and poetry. Unfortunately, nothing could divert her thoughts from the revelations in the study.

As the guests dispersed, Thomasse pulled Maud aside. "Can you discover the secrets of Lord Jack's past? I know Eleanor says he is honorable, but he is her brother."

Maud placed a hand on her arm. "Anything for you, my friend."

When the last of the guests had departed, Thomasse hastened to her chamber, a haven where she could nurse her wounds. Here, no one would dismiss her despair as childish.

Agnes helped Thomasse remove her gown and don her shift. "Why so forlorn?"

Thomasse flopped onto the bed. "Does my very countenance betray me?"

"Indeed. 'Tis plain for all to see." Agnes perched on the edge of the bed. "Come, unburden your cares."

"Oh, Agnes," Thomasse wailed, "Lady Eleanor is betrothed to Sir Arthur. How could my dearest friend wrong me thus?"

Agnes rubbed Thomasse's back. "Perchance it was not her decision. Maidens of her station often have no choice in whom they marry."

"There appeared to be more of an attachment than just an unexpected betrothal," Thomasse said, her throat tight. "But that is not the worst. I shall soon be bound in matrimony to Lady Eleanor's brother."

"Would it be so bad? Does he not have the same qualities as Sir Arthur—handsome, a large estate, and in favor with the king?"

"Yes, but—" Thomasse shuddered. "I know nothing of his character. I am certain he cares for naught but my dowry."

Agnes stroked her hair. "Surely, in time, he will come to care for you, and hopefully you him."

The maidservant rose and lumbered about the room, hanging the green gown in the wardrobe, stoking the fire, and straightening the combs, baubles, and jars on the dressing table. Her face was stoic, but Thomasse was not fooled. Agnes had been with her since she was a little girl, and her busyness belied her distress.

"What is it?" Thomasse asked.

"I hope Master Nicholas and Lord Jack will allow me to remain in your service."

Thomasse studied her maidservant, noticing the gray in her hair, her limp more pronounced, and her shoulders more stooped. She had aged so gradually over the years, Thomasse had not noticed until now. Indeed, Agnes's movements had slowed and her eyesight was failing. What a fearful prospect if she should need to seek a new position. "I will speak with my father."

Agnes curtsied. "Thank you, mistress. Now get some rest, there is early mass in the morn." She snuffed the candles and quit the room. The latch dropped into place, and footsteps shuffled down the hall.

Thomasse sat with her back against the bolster, and drew her knees to her chest as she contemplated Agnes's words. She longed for someone to acknowledge her feelings as just, that she had a right to be angry with Eleanor. But, as usual, Agnes spoke wise words.

What kind of friend was she if her first thought was that Eleanor had betrayed her? Perhaps Eleanor was merely accepting her fate as best she could—although judging by the looks that passed between her and Arthur, that seemed doubtful.

The fire crackled as Thomasse stared into the flames, irritated that her father had not informed her about Jack. Though she knew her father loved her, he rarely showed it any more. After her mother's death, he had grown distant, and after Richard, Duke of York, was killed in the battle at Wakefield, he had become increasingly distracted.

While she could appreciate the advantage to her father of aligning with an earl's family, had he once considered her needs? Devon was so far from their home here in Sussex. Far from everything and everyone that was familiar.

She sighed. The evening, which had begun with such promise, had ended in uncertainty. Sleep would not come easily.

# Chapter Two

Thomasse tossed and turned on her bed. In the ten days since the party, she had confined herself to her chamber, leaving only for morning prayers and vespers at the family chapel. Oft she sent her meals back to the kitchen untouched. Knowing Arthur could never be hers only made her heart pine for him all the more.

When her thoughts were not consumed by Arthur, she fretted about Jack. At his age, why was he not yet married? Had he been sent away to hush up a scandal? Was there a bastard child hidden somewhere? Or did he have a penchant for gambling? It was all so distressing.

Abandoning hope of sleep, she lit the candle beside the bed, and retrieved Maud's letter, hidden earlier beneath the bolster. She had read only the first line, for it promised no good tidings. Unable to delay knowing the truth any longer, she wrapped herself in a blanket and sat by the hearth to read it by the dwindling fire.

*Thomasse,*

*I pray this letter finds your spirits improved and that its contents will set your mind at ease, although it contains unsettling news.*

*My days are busy attending Queen Margaret, but I have found time to make inquiries at court. All speak highly of Lord John Courtenay. He was not sent away from home, but rather placed in service to the Percy family, common for boys of noble birth. His own father was a loyal knight who fought bravely for our king in the battle at St. Albans.*

*I do not mean to cause alarm, but my mind is deeply troubled. All morning, I watched the king's knights ride out to the north. Rumors abound that another battle looms between the houses of Lancaster and York. Every day I pray for peace and that our paths cross again soon.*

*Toujours amis, Maud*

Thomasse refolded the letter and returned it to its safe hiding place beneath the bolster. She crawled into bed, her fears about Jack assuaged.

The bliss of a long, elusive sleep had nearly found her when pounding on the outer door jarred her awake. Loud male voices could be heard below, and she wondered who had so rudely arrived at this late hour. Footfalls pounded on the stairs, followed by a rap on her chamber door.

"Wake up, Mistress Thomasse! Wake up!"

She rolled out of bed and padded to the door. "What is it, Agnes?" she asked, lifting the latch.

Her maidservant pushed past her into the room. "Master Nicholas says you must depart forthwith."

Thomasse followed Agnes about the room as she retrieved a satchel from the wardrobe and stuffed it with a kirtle, a woolen gown, and various items from the dressing table.

"What happened?" Thomasse asked. "I am not going anywhere in the middle of the night without a proper explanation."

"Make haste—the horses are being readied. Master Nicholas will explain on the way."

Not willing to defy her father, Thomasse relented and allowed Agnes to dress her in a sturdy cotehardie. "I am frightened," she whispered as the maidservant tightened the laces.

"Do not be. Your father always protects you. I pray you will be gone but a few days."

Thomasse threw herself into Agnes's arms and hugged her tightly.

Within the quarter hour, Thomasse was astride Freya, the dappled palfrey she received on her twelfth birthday. Clouds shrouded the half-moon as they rode out the gate of the estate. Her father rode up ahead with a half-dozen men-at-arms dressed in hauberks and coifs, lanterns held high, swords strapped at their sides. At her father's command, they encircled her as they rode southward.

The clouds thickened, the wind picked up, and the skies dumped heavy rains, leaving her drenched and cold. She gritted her teeth and wrapped her cloak more tightly around her, although it did little to dispel the chill that settled in her bones. In the stormy darkness, she feared her beloved horse might stumble and suffer injury. *What possessed Father to leave at such an inopportune time and in harsh weather?*

After nigh an hour, her father joined her.

"What is the meaning of this?" Thomasse asked. "What is so pressing you must drag me from my bed?"

"You wished to tour the Continent. The perfect time has presented," he said with a forced smile. "If we delay, we shall miss the boat."

"And my friends?"

"They will join us in Paris," he replied.

"But I have no proper clothes. And without Agnes, who will attend me?"

"All is arranged. You shall order new garments upon our arrival, and I shall retain a new maidservant. Now, no more questions." Her father nudged his steed forward, rejoining the circle of men.

After several hours of riding, the sun crept over the hills. Her father ordered his men to veer into a dense copse some distance from the road. There, they dismounted. Thomasse was grateful for the break for every muscle in her body ached. Once the horses were tied, the men removed sacks filled with bread, cheese, and leather costrels of ale. The victuals were passed around and quickly vanished. While the men cleaned up, her father instructed half the group to take the first watch while the others slept. The other half fetched blankets from their saddle bags and stretched out on the ground beneath the trees.

Thomasse's eyes widened when her father handed her a blanket. "Surely you do not expect me to sleep under the open sky like a mumble crust? Can we not take a room at an inn?"

His glare warned her to hold her tongue. "We must make the best of it. We have a few nights' journey ahead, so take your rest."

"Would it not be safer to travel by day?"

He settled down beside her and leaned against the tree. "I know what I am about."

Aware her father would accept no further argument, Thomasse retrieved her satchel to use as a pillow and pulled the blanket over her. The ground was hard; her bruised body conscious of every pebble. Despite her efforts, she could not get comfortable, and her body rebelled at the idea of slumbering in the day.

She struggled to make sense of what had happened over the last several hours. Her father's explanation seemed suspect. If they were truly travelling to the Continent, they would travel by day and in comfort. Travelling under cover of darkness on muddy roads was unsettling. The surreptitious manner of their journey made her feel they were fleeing. But why? What could they be running from?

Maud's letter spoke of an impending battle in the north. If so, why was her father not joining King Henry's forces. And only days earlier, her father had dismissed the planned tour of the Continent. Now, he acted as if everything were happening just as planned.

She bolted upright. "Tell me, Father, why do we hide as if someone were in pursuit?"

"Who put such nonsense in your head?"

"I heard rumors of a coming conflict in the north. You have always fought with King Henry, and yet we journey to the south."

"The battle is over. My concern is for your safety."

"My safety? What am I in danger from?"

"Brigands along the highway." Her father stood. "I refuse to discuss this with you any further." With that, he strode away and joined the men on the first watch.

Thomasse wrapped the blanket more tightly around her, trying to stave off the cold, still troubled by her father's explanation. The sudden departure seemed unnecessary. Finding no logical explanation, she hoped a warm meal, a hot bath, and a comfortable bed awaited, whatever the destination.

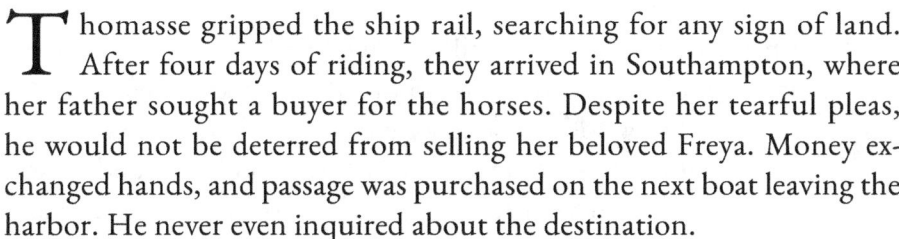

Thomasse gripped the ship rail, searching for any sign of land. After four days of riding, they arrived in Southampton, where her father sought a buyer for the horses. Despite her tearful pleas, he would not be deterred from selling her beloved Freya. Money exchanged hands, and passage was purchased on the next boat leaving the harbor. He never even inquired about the destination.

Waves slapped against the sides, and the ship rocked. She braced her feet to steady herself. This vessel held no comforts for a lady, no private quarters where she could wash or change out of her dirt-streaked cotehardie. She was certain bruises covered her body, and now, the constant wind had turned her hair into a mass of tangles.

It was unthinkable that she would step ashore in such a state of disarray. How much easier it would be to endure this humiliation if her friends were beside her to share the experience and buoy her confidence.

Loud voices captured her attention. Her father appeared to be in a heated confrontation with the captain. He threw up his hands and stalked over to her. "Fie on him!" he muttered. "I would run the arrogant bastard through with a sword, except the crew would toss us both overboard."

"What were you arguing about?" Thomasse asked.

"Nothing of consequence. When we reach the Continent, this will all be behind us."

The gale whipped her cloak away from her body, and she shivered. Ahead, a narrow shadow appeared. "Look!" She pointed eagerly. "Land! We are almost there." Soon she would be reveling in a warm bath.

The crew lowered the sails, and the ship slowed. "Grab your satchel," her father said, "we are leaving this ship."

Thomasse gasped. "That cannot be. We are still miles from land."

"They will lower a boat, and I will row us to shore."

She stared, at a loss for words. What did either of them know about rowing a boat through choppy winter waters? Or even smooth waters? The captain might as well hang them or toss them overboard. Those would be quicker deaths.

The crew lowered a small boat into the water and dropped a rope ladder down the side of the ship.

Her father patted her arm. "I shall go down first."

Thomasse clutched her satchel, watching in horror as her father began his descent. The flimsy ladder swayed with every step, his movements slow and deliberate. He carefully stepped into the boat as it pitched and twisted in the waves. "Drop your satchel," he called, his words barely discernable above the roar of the wind and waves.

She released it, holding her breath as it tumbled over and over and bounced off the rim of the boat. Her father leaned out and snatched it before the waves carried it away.

A lump formed in her throat as she stared down the side. It was so far down. She had no choice but to hike up her skirt and climb over the rail. Her face burned when two of the seamen stepped forward to assist her while the others watched.

She gripped the rail and cautiously lowered one foot, feeling for the first rung. Each downward step challenged her fortitude and strength as her cloak and skirt whipped wildly in the wind. She clung tighter to the ropes, fearful of losing her grip. Halfway down, her foot caught in her skirt. The fabric tore, and she felt herself slip. Her father quickly ascended the ladder and grabbed her foot, placing it firmly on the next rung.

He wrapped an arm around her waist, assisting her the rest of the way down the ladder, and settled her onto the seat in the boat.

Grabbing the oars, he began to row. Thomasse gripped the edges of the boat, heart in her throat as the waves crashed against the sides, sloshing water into the hull. Progress was slow as he battled the choppy waters, and a growing puddle formed in the bottom of the boat.

After what seemed like hours, the breaking waves slammed the boat into the rocks near the shore. "I cannot take us any further. You must wade the rest of the way in. I will push the boat out and paddle farther north where the shore is sandy and I can pull it from the water."

The boat tilted precariously when she dipped a foot in. She gasped and drew it back from the icy cold water, the spray from the crashing waves stinging her face. Taking a deep breath, she grabbed the satchel and stepped into the breakers.

With the oar, her father pushed the boat away from the rocks and rowed northward along the shoreline.

Her wet skirt clung to her legs. She took a step forward but stumbled backward as the waves receded. Fighting the pull of the undertow, she lost her balance and her grip on the satchel as she was dragged under. The waves tumbled her about until she could not tell which way was up or down. Her lungs burned; she needed air.

Her skirt and cloak twisted around her body so tightly she could move neither arms nor legs. She wriggled like a fish, hoping to get her head above water. Miraculously, someone or something lifted her from the water and set her on her feet. She coughed and sucked in several breaths. Another wave tugged at her skirt, and she tottered. The same strong arms scooped her up, carried her to shore, and set her on the sand.

"Thank you," Thomasse croaked as she pushed aside the hair plastered across her face and rubbed the water from her eyes. Her mouth tasted of salt. A short distance away, her father was dragging the boat ashore. She twisted around to see her rescuer.

Before her stood a man in his early twenties, wringing water from his gray tunic. His damp, shoulder-length hair hung limply about his face. Beautiful amber eyes, the color of warm honey, studied her face.

He said something, but his words were unintelligible.

An awkward silence hung between them. She was not fit to be seen, and sand was irritating her skin in unmentionable places. She scrambled backward, teeth chattering, "Who—Who are you?"

"Name is James," he replied, removing his coif.

"Thank you for saving my life."

"You need to get out of those wet clothes before you catch your death of cold," he said.

The import of his words took a few moments to register. "My satchel," she exclaimed, glancing out at the water just in time to see it bob on the waves and disappear beneath the surface. "Now what? I have no dry clothes to change into."

The corner of his mouth ticked. "None of them would have been dry." He whistled, and a roan mare trotted over. He opened the saddlebag and withdrew a grey, woolen blanket. "Let me wrap this around you."

Thomasse fumbled with the clasp of her cloak.

"Let me help." He made quick work of it. Gentle hands pushed the cloak from her shoulders and draped the blanket around her.

"There is a cottage nearby. I shall take you there."

Thomasse shook her head. "I do not mean to sound ungrateful, but I must wait for my father. He will know what to do."

"I shall accompany you. He may need my help. I doubt he is familiar with Jersey."

"What is Jersey?" she asked.

"'Tis an isle off the coast of Normandy," he replied, grabbing the roan's reins and leading the horse as they walked toward her father.

Her body shivered uncontrollably. "So we have not made it to the Continent?"

"It is but a few miles more, although it would take some time to row there in a cockboat."

She furrowed her brow. "The first thing you said—I could not understand it. Do people here speak a different tongue?"

He smiled. "Most of the isle folk speak Jèrriais. What is your name? And how have you come to wash up on our shores?"

"I am Mistress Thomasse. My father and I were sailing from England to the Continent when the captain put us off the ship in the middle of the Channel."

"How fortunate I was riding by," James said. As they neared her father, James lifted his hand to the side of his mouth and called out, "Would you like some help?"

Her father's head jerked up and he stared at James. She thought she saw a flicker of recognition, but it quickly vanished. "I can handle this myself."

When they reached him, Thomasse said, "Father, this is James. He rescued me from the water."

It was several moments before her father spoke, as he appeared to be composing himself. Perhaps he too felt the awkwardness of making a new acquaintance in his wet state. "I am obliged to you."

James pointed at a tiny house nestled between the hills. "With your permission, I would like to take your daughter to that cottage so she can get warm before a chill sets in."

Her father looked at her, then back at James. "A wise decision, as it will take some time to drag the boat over there."

James mounted the roan and lifted Thomasse into the saddle. He wrapped an arm about her waist and nudged the horse forward. She tensed. A proper maiden would object, but the warmth of his body took the edge off the chill.

This was different, she told herself. This was about survival. Besides, she sensed a gentleness about him that chased away her fear. She snuggled deeper into his arms.

The mare trotted across the sand until they reached the modest cottage. James dismounted, reached up, and caught her around the waist as he helped her down. She met his gaze, his eyes full of kindness and concern. A shyness crept over her, and she stepped back.

He strode toward the cottage. She smoothed her hair back from her face and followed him inside.

The cottage consisted of a single room, furnished with a decrepit plank table surrounded by four mismatched chairs, and a rickety sideboard cluttered with earthen vessels, wooden trenchers, and utensils. Beneath her feet, dry, dusty rushes crumbled. Outside, the wind whistled. James stepped to the lone window and closed the shutters.

Her eyes followed him as he moved about the cottage. He gathered a few logs from the stack near the door before searching for a flint.

"Who owns this place?" Thomasse asked.

"A fisher lived here, but he passed some years ago."

She glanced around. A fishing net covered in cobwebs hung on the wall near the door, and a couple of filthy bed mats rested in the far corner. "How far to the nearest inn?"

"About a half hour's walk."

Her mood darkened. There would be no hot bath, no warm meal, or even a comfortable bed tonight.

With the fire started, he headed for the door. "I will return with some dry clothes and victuals from the manor house."

"Thank you."

James inclined his head and slipped outside.

Thomasse pulled out a chair and ran a finger through the thick layer of dust on the back. No one could have lived here for years. Too tired to care about the dirt, she sat down, shrugged off the blanket, and removed her wet boots and stockings. She struggled with the sodden laces of her cotehardie and let it slip to the floor. She draped it across the back of a chair to dry and drew it over to the fire. Wearing only a thin kirtle, she stretched her hands to the fire, soaking in the warmth, hoping her father would arrive soon.

## Chapter Three

James vaulted onto the roan and scanned the beach. Thomasse's father was still some distance from the cottage, dragging the cockboat across the sand. The man's clothes were soaked and torn, his wet hat and hair plastered to his head. After rowing through rough waters, he must be exhausted.

James rode over. "My offer still stands."

Her father dropped the cockboat and wiped his brow. "No need. It is not much farther."

The man's resistance to his kind gesture piqued James's curiosity. If it was a matter of stubborn pride, he did not wish to press the matter. "Thomasse warms herself by the fire. I will bring food later."

"Your generosity is admirable." From the man's accent, it was apparent he was a member of the English gentry.

"Might I inquire your name, sir?" James asked.

Her father looked back toward the bay, avoiding James's gaze. "Why do you need to know?"

"No particular reason. I know everyone around these parts, and you are new here."

Clearing his throat, the man said, "Call me Nicholas."

James frowned. After suffering such misfortune, why did the man behave as if he, James, was a threat? Something must be amiss, in which case questioning him further would be futile.

"Pleased to make the acquaintance." James touched his coif. "You are certain I cannot lend a hand?"

Nicholas grabbed the rim of the cockboat, struggling to get it moving again. "As I said before, I will do it myself."

"As you wish," James replied.

He wheeled the roan about and urged the horse forward, cantering across the sand and up the path over the hillock behind the cottage. As he rode, he pondered Nicholas's strange behavior. The sense of distrust did not square with a man allowing a stranger to ride off with his daughter. For a moment, James had thought Nicholas recognized him. If so, James did not recall having met the man before, but then it would have been under very different circumstances.

James's thoughts returned to Thomasse, recalling the feel of her body nestled in his arms. It had been nigh two years since he had held a woman so close. Despite her scent of salt water and seaweed, it felt good.

The familiar ache grew as memories of Becca surfaced, but he shoved them aside. It had taken so much inner strength to heal after losing her—he could not let some drowning maiden threaten that.

When he arrived at the stable, he found Seigneur de Carteret brushing down his prized destrier, Magnar—a magnificent black warhorse.

The seigneur glanced up. "James, at last. I had begun to worry."

"I spotted a cockboat in trouble. I reached the shore just in time to save a lady from drowning," he said, as he dismounted the roan. "An English damsel and her father have come ashore. There was a ship just beyond the bay. She said the captain put them off. Some mischief must be afoot, for who would abandon passengers in the midst of the Channel?"

"Odd, indeed." De Carteret stroked the destrier's nose. "Did they offer any details?"

"Very little, although they are certainly not of the common folk. The man gave the name of Nicholas. There was a moment when I thought he recognized me, but I cannot place him."

De Carteret set aside the brush and leaned against the stall door. "Nicholas, you say? Did you bring them to the manor house?"

James shook his head. "They are at my cottage. Since I no longer live there, I saw no harm in letting them stay a night or two. Given the recent invasion by the French, I hesitate to bring strangers to the house. The safety of your family is my primary concern."

De Carteret clapped James on the shoulder. "Your caution is well placed. The chaos of this occupation consumes all my time. I suspect there is much more to their story. I will depend on you for that. Take them victuals from the cookhouse. We do not want them starving."

"Certainly not," James replied. "Perhaps they will be more open to questioning upon my return."

"You have my full confidence," de Carteret said, as he quit the stable and headed toward the manor house.

Gratified by the seigneur's trust, James gathered supplies for the newcomers. Heading to the back corner of the stable, his step faltered. There, he had stashed away a small box, nearly forgotten now. He gathered his courage and moved aside an old saddle and pitchfork and pulled it out.

He opened the lid and drew out Becca's blue cotehardie and shook it out. Her brush slipped to the ground and lay at his feet. He pressed the worn blue wool, softened from wear, against his cheek, before stooping to retrieve the brush. He ran his finger across the carving on the back—flowers, leaves, and hearts—remembering how he had lovingly made it for her as a wedding gift. Could he let them go? These were all he had left of her.

# Chapter Four

Thomasse rubbed her arms and stamped her feet, trying to get warm. The blanket James had left behind helped stave off the chill, but only slightly.

Her father appeared in the doorway, his clothes soaked and caked with sand, his brow glistening with sweat. "I got the boat up to the cottage. We may need it again."

Her brow furrowed. "I hope not."

He scanned the cottage, his gaze lighting on the woodpile. Selecting a log, he tossed it onto the fire. Soon, smoke billowed, filling the room.

Thomasse coughed, and her eyes stung. "Can we not find an inn? This place is not fit for a dog."

"I am too tired to seek lodging," her father said, as he threw open the shutters.

Through the open door, she spied James coming down the hill, leading an ass laden with baskets.

"Quick!" Thomasse grabbed the still damp cotehardie. "James is coming. Help me dress."

Her father helped pull the garment over her head. By the time James arrived in the doorway, she was properly dressed.

James entered carrying two parcels and a jug, and set them on the table.

Thomasse opened the first one and withdrew two woolen blankets, a grey tunic, black hose, a patched kirtle, and a blue cotehardie. The worn wool felt soft against her skin. She shook it out, and a brush dropped onto the floor. She retrieved it, admiring the fine carving on the back. "How beautiful! This was most thoughtful."

James's eyes dulled, and his voice cracked. "It belonged to—my wife."

24

"I am so sorry." She clasped the brush to her breast, realizing the gift had cost him. "I promise to treasure it."

Her father opened the second parcel, which contained a loaf of bread, a lump of cheese, and some dried fruit.

Thomasse eyed the victuals. Her stomach gnawed, an unfamiliar sensation. At the moment, all she could think of was stuffing bits of fruit and chunks of bread in her mouth. But proper manners restrained her. She would not deign to behave like a vagabond. After all, she was a daughter of the gentry, soon to be betrothed to the son of an earl.

The ass brayed. James stepped outside and returned with a large kettle filled with vegetables and a bucket. "Everything you need to prepare a nice stew."

"We will repay you for your trouble," her father said.

"No need. The victuals are compliments of Seigneur de Carteret and his family."

Her father's face paled, and something akin to fear flickered in his eyes.

*How could a kind gesture cause dread?* Thomasse wondered.

James met Thomasse's gaze. "Might I ask what part of England you hail from?"

"Perchance we can answer your questions another time," her father replied, his words clipped. "We are quite tired from our journey."

James gave a brief nod. "If you need anything, I will come by on the morrow." At the door, he glanced back at Thomasse. "Sleep well."

Once the door was shut and barred, Thomasse grabbed the bread and tore off a large portion, handing the rest to her father. She shoved several pieces in her mouth, trying to drive away the hunger. She lifted the jug of ale and drank until her throat was no longer parched, uncaring of her father's disapproving look. Sated, she sat beside the fire to brush out her tangled tresses.

"You were rather rude, Father," said Thomasse. "James seems a nice sort, and it was very kind of him to bring us food and dry garments."

"God's teeth! One cannot be too careful around strangers." Her father looked at her askew. "Tell me you do not have your eyes on a new beau when you are nigh betrothed. Beware, lest you confuse gratitude with regard."

"It is only natural to be curious. He saved my life. Do you think he is the seigneur's son?"

"He is the groom."

Her face warmed. How had she missed the clues—the ill-fitting tunic, the scuffed boots? "So you do know him? Why did you not acknowledge it before?"

He rose from the table, snatched a blanket, and picked up a mat. "We met briefly once in London." Unfolding the mat, he laid it out before the fire and drew the blanket over him. "I am too tired to answer any more questions tonight."

Yawning, she continued to brush her unruly locks. If they had been home, Agnes would do this for her. A tear slid down her cheek. Faced with everything that had happened the last several days, how silly that only this had made her cry.

She laid the brush aside and pulled the other filthy mat over to the fire. Tomorrow she would clean the cottage, but tonight she needed sleep. Although humble, at least there was a roof over their heads.

In her dreams, she was in the garden of their home in Sussex, walking hand-in-hand with a tall man. He drew her close, his hand firm, yet gentle. She lifted her face, awaiting his kiss. Their eyes met. But they did not belong to Arthur—or Jack. They were amber. Startled, she awoke, her heart racing.

Had Agnes and her father been right? Were her affections so fleeting?

She tossed and turned, willing sleep to return, her mind disturbed as she tried to grasp the significance. Dreams were strange things, weaving together memories and imaginations—but always with meaning.

Light filtered through the cracks in the shutters, waking Thomasse. Every muscle in her body ached, and she wondered if the bruises and tenderness would ever go away. Yet she must confess, sleeping on the thin mat with a roof over her head was preferable to bare, wet ground beneath the sky.

She rolled over. Her father's mat was empty. He sat at the table, dressed in the gray tunic and black hose, inspecting the fishing net.

Thomasse sat up and stretched. "Good morning, Father."

He grumbled something she could not make out.

Scrambling up, she joined him. "What are you doing?"

He waved a hand over the net. "Trying to figure this thing out. I have never fished with a net before. Thought I might try my hand."

"To what purpose?"

"You know I can never bear to be idle." He scooped up the net and tossed it onto his shoulder. "I shall return in a few hours."

When he had gone, she removed the garments from the parcel James had delivered the evening before. Although worn, at least they were not torn. She slipped the cotehardie over her head and drew in the laces. Digging through the pile of discarded garments, she rescued her stockings and pulled them on. Her boots were still damp, but given the circumstances, she was grateful to have them at all.

Her stomach rumbled, followed by pangs of hunger. She grabbed the remainder of the bread, tossing it aside when she could not bite through it. Unfortunately, stale and hard, it was only fit for feeding the swine.

Upon searching the cottage, she found nothing with which to clean it other than the bucket. With nothing to occupy her hands and no one to talk to, she ventured outside.

Overhead, gulls soared and shrieked, and the salt air smelled fresh after the smoky cottage. She climbed to the crest of the hillock behind the humble dwelling. To the west lay an endless expanse of water; to the south, the green hills were dotted with grazing sheep; and to the north, the sandy shore gave way to rocky cliffs.

Looking eastward, a stream wound lazily through a grove of alder trees just beyond the base of the hillock. To the south stood the family chapel, and a bit farther on, what appeared to be a stable. To the north was a cookhouse with a brick oven out front. Two men were pulling bread from it, the aroma wafting on the breeze made her mouth water.

Across the green sat the manor house built of brown stone. Not a grand structure like their home in Sussex, but compared to the modest cottage, it looked like a mansion. A group of soldiers dressed in blue tunics gathered near the door.

She sat beneath a tree in the grove and watched two lads fighting with wooden swords on the green. They were of similar age, one with dark shoulder-length hair, the other with sandy locks. *These must be the seigneur's sons.* Maybe there were other children her age, a daughter perchance, whom she could befriend.

The door of the manor house opened and two soldiers walked out and joined the others. Together, they strode toward the stables and soon were riding away down the pathway.

She turned back to watch the boys who had finished their game. They hurtled in her direction. She sprang up and ducked behind the tree, embarrassed by her faded attire.

They sat on the crest of the hill and chattered like monkeys. "One day, I will be a knight like my father," the dark-haired boy said.

"Not me. I intend to own a ship and sail the world," the lanky, sandy-haired lad replied.

The dark-haired boy punched the other in the arm. "Impossible, William. You shall be reeve when I am seigneur."

William shrugged. "What is wrong with dreaming of bigger things?"

"We cannot always get what we want," the dark-haired boy replied. "After my sister died, I wished for another sibling, but my prayers were never answered."

That told her all she needed to know. There were no children her age at the manor. A branch cracked behind her, and she whirled about, slamming into something hard. She stumbled backward.

A firm hand grabbed her arm. "My apologies. I did not mean to startle you. I was just heading to the cottage to see if you needed anything." She glanced up to find a wide grin and amber eyes alight with amusement. "I see the clothes fit," James said.

Her face heated at the memory of last night's dream. "They will suffice until I get new gowns," she replied primly.

A twisted smile replaced his grin. He pivoted and strode back toward the stable.

Her cheeks burned. How ungrateful she must sound! She owed him so much—her life, last night's supper, even the clothes she wore. But should she beg his pardon?

She had been taught common folk lacked the sensibilities of gentlefolk, but his reactions spoke of emotions that ran deep.

Unwilling to leave things as they were, she hastened after him. "James, wait."

He did not slow his pace as she followed him to the stable, chiding herself for her rudeness.

"Will you show me the horses?" she asked timidly.

He handed her some parsnips from the basket near the door.

She wandered down the row of stalls, admiring the horses, stroking their noses, and offering them treats. "I had a dappled palfrey until a few days ago. Her name was Freya."

"That explains your ease around horses."

An awkward pause stretched between them. Thomasse broke the silence. "I noticed a group of soldiers leaving earlier. Is it too presumptuous to ask why they were here?"

"Jersey was recently invaded by the French. I suspect their presence is something to which we must become accustomed."

Without warning, a black hound bounded around the corner. He jumped up and licked her face. Thomasse shrank back against the stall door.

"Down, Puddles." James's voice was firm. Glancing at Thomasse, he said, "He will not hurt you."

Puddles gazed up at her with innocent eyes.

"You two have just met, but it appears Puddles is already enamored with you." James gave the dog a playful shove. "Move along, boy, I saw her first."

Thomasse laughed. "I am flattered. A maiden enjoys having men vie for her attention now and then." She tapped her temple. "How shall I choose between you?"

The twinkle returned to James's eyes. "A pity if I lost out to a dog, but it would not be the first time." He ducked around the corner and returned with a towel. "I know 'tis for the horses, but it will do the trick."

As she wiped the slobber from her cheek, her stomach rumbled.

His brow wrinkled. "Have you eaten today?" When Thomasse shook her head, he continued. "Go ask for food at the cookhouse."

"It would not be proper. I have yet to meet the seigneur and his family."

"Our seigneur keeps an open door. Strangers are welcome to dine without invitation." He offered her his arm. "You can go alone, or, if it makes you more comfortable, I can accompany you there. However, I cannot stay. Will you be able to find your way home?"

"I hope so." A vision of her comfortable chamber at their home in Sussex rose in her mind. "I sincerely hope so."

Her hunger satisfied, Thomasse returned to the cottage. From the doorway, she spotted her father, his hair windblown and clothes disheveled, dragging the boat across the sand. From a distance, he looked like any other fisher. She ran to meet him. "Did you catch anything?"

"Unfortunately, no." His shoulders were stooped, his walk unsteady. "It is harder than it looks. I tried asking for help, but I cannot understand a word these fishers say."

"Certainly, you will fare better tomorrow."

They walked the remaining distance to the cottage in silence. Inside, her father flung himself into a chair while Thomasse opened the shutters to let in more light.

The sun shining directly through the window revealed thick layers of grime covering the worn furniture and the dishes and utensils stacked on the rickety sideboard. Thomasse cringed. The place was scarcely habitable.

She was grateful that Eleanor and Maud were travelling separately, and did not have to endure such indignities.

On the table sat a hemp sack containing a variety of vegetables and a loaf of bread. James must have brought them while she was at the cookhouse. "I guess I need to learn to cook." She pulled out a roundish green item, eyeing it with suspicion. "I do not even know what this is?"

"I believe it is a cabbage," her father replied. His eyes drooped. "Consider this part of your adventure."

She removed the remaining vegetables; onions, garlic, parsnips, a variety of beans, and a lone turnip. "I thought adventures were supposed to be fun."

He managed a wry smile that did not reach his eyes. "It is all in your perspective. This is bound to be short-lived, so let us enjoy pretending to be peasants."

"Let us hope so."

"Once King Henry ar—" He cut himself off, lips pressed tight.

"What do you mean?"

"I have said too much already. Nothing to concern yourself with." He crossed his arms. "Now, we were discussing supper."

Knowing she would get nothing more from him, she fetched the bucket beside the door. "I discovered a stream just over the hill. If you tend the fire, I will fetch water."

She loaded two bowls, spoons, and cups into the bucket. Then added a knife and a ladle before heading out the door.

When she reached the crest of the hillock, the manor's supper horn blew. Peasants and a few soldiers in their blue tunics converged on the manor from every direction. She was grateful for the privacy while she washed the dishes; it spared her the humiliation of being seen doing servants' work.

She plunged her hands into the icy stream, scraping at the hardened-on bits of dried food with her fingernails. When finished, she filled the bucket with fresh water and trudged back over the hillock to the cottage. Her hands, red from the cold, stung as they warmed.

A fire blazed in the center of the floor, and a smoky haze hung over the room. Her eyes itched and watered. She coughed. It was hard to determine what was worse, the chilly air outside or the acrid air within. "Something must be wrong. Surely people do not live like this?"

"Just be thankful for a roof over your head." Something was different in his tone and demeanor, whether wistful or resigned, she was unsure. But she could not shake the feeling that he was hiding something.

# Chapter Five

Thomasse gazed about the cottage; a smile tugged at her lips as she recalled its state when they arrived on Jersey a fortnight ago. The stone walls, the sideboard and rickety table with four mismatched chairs, and the hearth in the center remained unchanged. However, the stench of rodents and dusty rushes, along with the cobwebs and filth, had been cleaned away. Although it contained nothing of beauty, after days of scrubbing, using rags made from her tattered cotehardie, the air smelled pleasantly of fresh-cut rushes and the wood gleamed. She hung the kettle filled with freshly chopped vegetables over the fire. Even her cooking had improved.

Her father arrived holding a couple of small fishes which he laid on the table to be cleaned.

"Father, I have been meaning to ask. How long until we sail for France?"

He dropped into a chair and sighed heavily. "I cannot say."

She groaned. "Lady Eleanor and Lady Maud must be frantic worrying what has become of us."

"No need to fuss; they never left England."

"What? You said—"

"I said what was needed to get you to leave that night," her father said, his tone casual.

"You lied to me!" Thomasse said, her voice rising. "And now I am living like a peasant. I wish I had never begged for a tour. I wish we were home."

"You are in luck. We are home."

Her mouth gaped. "That is not funny."

"Indeed, I am sincere." His face showed no sign of jest.

"Can we not return to England?" she asked.

"That would be unwise. I have made some dangerous enemies."

She dropped into a chair, determined this time to get answers. "If our stay is to be of some duration—"

"It is only until King Henry and his family arrive. Then, we will join them."

"You are not speaking sense." She eyed her father suspiciously. "It seems improbable they would come given the occupation by the French."

"The garrison is under the command of Queen Margaret's cousin."

"Ah! But why would the royal family come to an isle of little import to the kingdom?"

He stepped over to the window and peered out. "Jersey is a safe haven."

"And—why would the king of England need a safe haven?" A chill rippled through her body. "What are you not telling me?"

He shook his head. "It is better if you do not know."

"Father, look at me." She waited, but he kept his eyes averted. "If I must live this way, I deserve to know why."

"King Henry has been dethroned. The royal family has fled into exile."

"Nonsense. The Duke of York was killed in battle during the Christmas holy days."

"The father, yes. It is his son Edward who sits on the throne."

Her hands gripped the chair seat as she recalled the jubilation of Twelfth Night, when the good tidings arrived of Richard Plantagenet's death. Those loyal to the House of Lancaster had won a glorious victory at Wakefield. With the death of the Duke of York, she had believed the strife between the cousins was over. Clearly, she was ignorant of these matters.

"But why did we flee? Certainly King Edward would pardon you for remaining loyal."

Her father flinched. "That may be true for some, but I doubt he will grant me such benevolence."

"Why ever not?"

Her father traced a crack in the shutter. "Edward will not be so kind to those that hoisted his father's head over the gate at York. My estate has been seized, and we are penniless."

"But the horses, my beautiful Freya. You must have money from selling them."

His shoulders sagged, and he spoke barely above a whisper. "All gone. Needing a quick sale, I could not ask the best price. The ship's captain demanded a hefty sum for passage and his silence. But I believe we are safe here. I have been careful to avoid anyone I might know. Once King Henry and Queen Margaret arrive, they will raise an army. When they reclaim the throne, what is rightfully mine will be restored."

"But to live like peasants? Surely you must know a seigneur that will take us in."

"I know a few, but we are in days of shifting loyalties. It is no secret that Seigneur de Carteret of St. Ouen's Manor supports the Yorkists. He housed Edward of York and the Earl of Warwick whilst they were in exile. It is far more prudent not to take the risk."

"And if the royal family does not come?"

He shrugged.

Thomasse leaned back and closed her eyes. How could this be? Her future rested on the success of Margaret d'Anjou in ousting Edward from the throne, for nothing could depend on the rightful, but insane, King Henry. All the turmoil had begun on account of his inability to rule.

Meanwhile, they needed money to live. She must find work. A fearful prospect given she possessed no skills anyone would wish to pay for. She looked at her hands. They were already red and blistered, her nails ragged, from scrubbing the cottage. She did not have the sturdy build to labor in the fields. God forbid.

"How could you do this to me?"

"It was not my intent." He strode towards the door, slamming a chair against the table as he passed, and stalked out of the cottage.

Sinking to the floor, she sobbed. How dare he be angry with her when he was to blame for their awful plight. Her stomach twisted as the weight of their difficulty sank in. His actions may have condemned her to a life of servitude, working every day for food just to survive. How she longed for Agnes's comforting arms.

Ere long, she realized no one was listening to her fit of temper or even cared. Wallowing in self-pity would not rectify her father's mistakes or return them to their previous life. Nor would it cook their dinner. She wiped the tears away with her sleeve, determined not to let their new circumstances win. Despite her change in status, she was still a gentleman's daughter.

She set about making supper. Gritting her teeth, she picked up the knife. Still repulsed by their slimy scales and squishy innards, she flayed and filleted the fish and tossed them into the kettle before laying the table.

With no one to turn to for solace, loneliness weighed heavily on her heart. Unbidden, her thoughts turned to James. At least one person had shown them kindness.

Her heart fluttered at the thought of seeing him again. *God's bones, Thomasse. Get ahold of yourself. The man is beneath you.*

It was dark when her father returned. They ate supper in silence. When the meal was finished, her father excused himself and was soon snoring on his mat.

She retrieved the brush James had given her and began combing out her tresses; the tangles caught in the bristles. In the past, Agnes had always done this; but, perhaps, never again. Her heart felt hollow wondering what would become of her beloved maidservant.

She glanced down at the worn blue cotehardie. What would Eleanor and Maud say if they could see her now? Would they shun her? Oh, what did it matter if she would never see them again.

Thomasse paused to remove long blond strands from the bristles. It was as if with each stroke of the brush, it was ripping away the remnants of her old life.

# Chapter Six

By the time Thomasse awoke the next morning, her father had already gone. How could she remain angry with him when he rose before dawn each day to fish, just to keep food on the table? He was doing his best given their new circumstances.

Unfortunately, his catches did not leave enough to sell in the market. His lack of success made it necessary for her to find work. Not wanting to injure his pride, she had not spoken of it. Being thus debased could not be easy for him. But hunger and a desire to survive spurred a person to do things previously unthinkable.

She dressed quickly and headed over the hillock, hoping James might be of help. She found him brushing down the beautiful black stallion. The horse snorted and stamped when she entered the stable. James glanced up, his expression worried. "Is something amiss?"

She fumbled with the laces of her cotehardie, unable to meet his gaze. She never dreamed she would need to do something like this, and she needed to gather her courage. "I come for a favor. My father and I cannot continue to live off your generosity. Do you know where I might find work?" When James did not answer immediately, she turned to leave. "Pay no heed. It was wrong of me to ask."

"Look at me," James said, softly. She looked back and met his gaze. "Work is not something to be ashamed of. My mother could use another spinster."

Thomasse wrung her hands, embarrassed by the need to admit her own inadequacy. "I know nothing of spinning."

James smiled. "My mother is a patient teacher."

Thomasse relaxed and timidly returned his smile. "And it is better than toiling in the field."

"Indeed. When I finish grooming Magnar, I shall take you to her."

She settled onto the bench near the door to wait. James whispered to the high-strung stallion as he placed the halter over its head. She watched, fascinated by the deftness of his hands and his connection with the horse. But then she began to notice other things—the wave of his brown hair, the ripple of his muscles beneath his tunic as he strapped on the saddle. She looked away when he gathered the reins and led the horse from the stable, not wanting him to know she had been staring.

Outside, she heard the murmur of male voices. Unable to suppress her curiosity, she peeked around the door. James was assisting a man onto the stallion. The stranger's face was well-favored, his bearing and fine garments bespoke his nobility. Given James's deference, he must be the seigneur of the manor. She ducked back behind the wall, her thoughts whirling.

As a gentlewoman, work among the common folk could only be a temporary solution. If she and her father never returned to England, this man might prove an important connection—perhaps even the key to securing her future by finding a suitable husband among the isle's landed gentry.

James reappeared and beckoned her to follow. He closed the stable door and pointed out a path. "This one leads to the village."

They meandered along the path, passing flocks of sheep grazing on the low hills. A tall alder tree shaded the green where the fields gave way to the village. Ahead, several women holding clay pots were lined up at the well, and just beyond lay the mill. The curve in the road hid a row of gray stone houses to the left, and various establishments on the right.

The clang of the blacksmith's hammer mixed with the acrid smell of molten metal and burning wood. The aroma of roasting meat and brewing ale drifted into the street from the tavern, along with bursts of laughter and the hum of conversation.

Along the roadside, a man pulled fresh-baked bread from a brick oven, while a woman stood nearby with baskets of vegetables for sale.

The door of the cottage at the end of the street stood open. Several women and young girls chattered noisily in Jèrriais as they worked. Her heart sank. How was she to fit into a world where she did not belong?

A tall woman in a gray kirtle and yellow apron broke from the group. A blue scarf covered her hair, and her amber eyes matched James's. They spoke at length. Thomasse understood nothing beyond her name, but she admired the kindness and respect James showed his mother.

After several minutes, James said, "Thomasse, meet my mother, Colette."

"Welcome," Colette said in English, and motioned for Thomasse to join the others.

She glanced nervously at James.

He lightly touched her shoulder. "I leave you in capable hands. I shall return later to walk you home."

She stared at the door for several moments after he left, her nerves jangling. The one person she felt she could depend on was gone. She would prove she could learn a new skill, so he would not regret his decision. This would not be easy, given the language barrier. But what other choice did she have?

James strode down the village road to the pathway leading back to St. Ouen's Manor. His thoughts lingered on the maiden he had just left behind. Her request surprised him, something he would not have expected from the young lady he had rescued a fortnight ago.

Her appearance today, dressed in his wife's clothes, had been like a dagger to the heart. He had thought enough time had passed, that those feelings had been buried forever. It was more than just regret and remorse—but guilt over how drawn he was to Thomasse. For the first time in almost two years, he felt the urge to protect and care for someone—her.

He tried to shake the thoughts from his head, reminding himself of his solemn vow never to let his heart become involved again. He would attribute these feelings to compassion for a newcomer who had suffered misfortune.

The horses nickered when he opened the stable door. He fed each a parsnip, then threw himself into mucking out stalls. Just what he needed. Toil and the aroma of horse dung would clear his head.

When his work was finished for the day, he made the half-hour walk back to his mother's cottage.

He leaned against the doorjamb and watched Thomasse work. Dropping the spindle, she gave it a whirl, trying to twist the wool fibers into thread. Each time, it wobbled and slowed. His lips twitched, marveling at her perseverance. Despite her evident frustration, she refused to give up.

The bells of St. Ouen's Parish Church tolled, signaling the end of the workday. The women gathered their supplies and stored them in baskets before quitting the cottage.

Thomasse was the last to put away her tools. Her eyes were dull, her shoulders rounded, and her expression tense.

"Are you ready?" James asked.

She huffed and, pushing past him, marched up the street. He furrowed his brow and jogged to catch up to her. They walked the path from the village mostly in silence, Thomasse not saying a word in response to his questions.

Finally, he asked, "Have I caused some offence?"

She tossed her head. "If you must know, my hands are stiff and my back aches. I tried my best. And you find that amusing."

"Indeed I do not. I admire your determination."

She stopped and whirled to face him. "I may not be good with a spindle, but I have other skills. I can read and write."

"Fine skills," James replied, "although they have no application to spinning."

She lifted her chin and continued down the path. "Whatever you think, I am determined. If I can learn to read and write, I can learn to spin."

"I have full faith in you, otherwise I never would have brought you there."

Her face softened. "No one has said that to me before. It means a lot."

The path turned, and the manor house came into view. She touched his arm. "Thank you. I can find my way home from here." She ambled down the path leading up the hillock toward the bay-side cottage. When she reached the crest, the breeze caught her skirt, revealing shapely ankles and calves.

His arm still tingled where she had touched it. Dare he admit how much he had enjoyed her company? It was as if her touch had cracked the protective wall he had so carefully built. He could not allow it. Such an opening could put his heart in danger.

# Chapter Seven

J ames stormed down the hillock toward the bay-side cottage. *What was Thomasse thinking?* Had he considered her a cumberground, he would never have brought her to his mother. And yet, on her second day, she had failed to present for work.

When he reached the cottage, the cockboat was gone. At least her father had the good sense to rise and go about his business. He rapped on the door. Silence. A short distance away, swords rattled, followed by a deep laugh. Soldiers patrolling the shores, on the lookout for English warships. His ire turned to unease. Had she met some misfortune?

He knocked again. With still no response, he tried the door, and found it barred. "Thomasse, are you in there?"

Rushes crackled, and a sleepy voice said, "Who is it?"

"James."

Scuffling noises sounded within, then footsteps neared the door. "What do you want?" Her voice was raspy from sleep.

"I must speak with you forthwith."

"I am not dressed."

"Make haste." He pulled a block of wood and a small knife from his pouch and settled beneath the alder tree a few paces from the cottage to wait.

As he whittled, the face of a horse with a flowing mane emerged. Glancing up, he noted the sun was high overhead. "Fie!" Apparently, the maiden had no sense of time. Why had he bothered helping some spoiled daughter of the gentry?

As the tail emerged, the door creaked open and Thomasse appeared, her blond braid hanging over her shoulder—just the way Becca used to wear her hair. James sucked in his breath, pushing the memory aside.

She marched over and stood before him, hands on her hips. "It is improper for a man to call on a maiden when her father is not at home."

He gaped. "This is not a social call. My mother expected you this morning."

She tilted her head, her forehead wrinkled. "I did not realize I was under an obligation."

James clenched his jaw as he shoved the carved figure and knife back into his pouch. "Unlike your privileged life, we common folk do not have the luxury of showing up only when it suits."

Thomasse nibbled her lip. Her mouth opened as if to speak, but she closed it again.

"I am happy to see you are not trying to excuse your behavior."

"I slept poorly last night." She raised her hands, showing him her palms. "How can I be expected to work with blisters?"

James rose and brushed the sand from his tunic. "Would you have accepted that excuse if a servant failed to rise early to stoke the fires or empty the chamber pots?"

"That is different," Thomasse replied.

"How?"

She blinked rapidly, but offered no response.

"Precisely. This, after I persuaded my mother to take you on. Your blunder will be the gossip of the village. No one will deign to employ you after such a misstep."

A flush darkened her cheeks. "But without work, we will starve."

"Perhaps you will think about that next time you decide to be a lie-abed."

She looked like a frightened child, her big blue eyes glistening like the bay on a beautiful summer day. "Can you explain to your mother it was a misunderstanding?"

His anger dissolved as he contemplated her difficult situation, trying to adjust to her new way of life, although he refused to be taken in by her shameless attempt at guile. "You must speak on your own behalf. Leaning on me will make you look weak."

"But you will go with me? Please!" She reached out and touched his arm. "I need an advocate. Your mother speaks little English and I no Jèrriais."

"If she agrees to take you back, promise this will never happen again."

"I give you my word."

"Be forewarned—my mother does not easily forgive." Without waiting for her, he headed up the hill.

T homasse lifted her skirt to keep from stumbling as she tried to keep pace with James. She regretted disappointing him. Nonetheless, she was grateful he would be with her when she faced his mother's wrath. Never in her life had she dreaded an impending conversation. How could she have displayed such folly?

It was humiliating enough that she needed to seek work, but now she needed to beg to keep it. Her survival, and that of her father, might rest on the success of her plea to Colette for mercy. She reminded herself, better to suffer shame now than be reduced to begging along the roadside or seeking help at the almshouse.

Thomasse's steps slowed as they neared the cottage. "Do you think Colette will give me another chance?"

James shrugged. "I cannot say. She was greatly vexed. I suggest showing penitence and confessing your wrongdoing."

Thomasse smoothed the skirt of the blue cotehardie and pushed her braid behind her shoulder. Colette scowled at the sight of her. When the other women began to whisper, she barked a few words, and they quickly resumed spinning.

Colette stood, her legs firmly planted as she spoke with James, pointing toward the door. He listened quietly until she finished.

He replied in a hushed tone, and Colette calmed. Thomasse wished she understood what they were saying. Finally, he addressed her. "My mother has agreed to listen to your explanation."

Thomasse dipped her head. "Give Colette my apologies. I beg her forgiveness for my ignorance." She showed Colette her palms. "I thought myself unfit to be of use."

James translated for his mother, who shook her head. "She refuses to accept your explanation. All her spinsters have suffered the same, so 'tis no excuse for your willful absence."

"Tell her I promise never to miss again."

After another exchange, James relayed Colette's response. "She says begone, that we are wasting her time."

Unbidden, tears leaked from Thomasse's eyes. She dropped to the ground and grabbed Colette's hand. "I beg you to reconsider. Is there no mercy in your Christian heart for a stranger?"

James relayed the message. Had her words been enough? As he continued speaking, she wondered if he was pleading on her behalf. Colette's face softened, and she nodded.

"She agrees to give you one more chance. Do not disappoint her for she will not relent again."

Thomasse rose. "Thank you, James. I shall repay this kindness."

She hurried over and retrieved the distaff and spindle from the basket, fumbling and dropping it. As she stooped to pick it up, she saw James disappear out the door.

The women, who had smiled and tried to be helpful yesterday, glared their disapproval. Thomasse kept her eyes on her work. *I will not cry. What do I need of them?* "I can do this," she whispered to herself over and over.

The afternoon passed slowly, and by the time the bells tolled, Thomasse could hardly move. She laid away her tools and the poorly made thread in the basket, noting how the other spinsters' work was far superior and in greater quantity. It was strange to feel lacking compared to common folk.

Halfway down the path to St. Ouen's Manor, footfalls sounded behind her.

"I hope all went well," James said as he caught up.

"Thank you again for interceding for me."

He frowned. "Do not make me regret it."

Thomasse smiled shyly. "I fear the alternative."

When they crested the hillock, Thomasse bid him farewell. At the door, she turned back and waved. James waved back, then disappeared behind the hillock.

Inside, her father sat at the table examining the fishing net.

"I believe I have discovered the problem." He lifted a portion of the net. "There is a small hole. Might I impose upon your womanly skills to mend it?"

Thomasse examined the net. "How do you propose I do that?"

Her father shrugged. "I know nothing of these things. Someone at least taught you needlework."

"But I was never proficient. Even if I had thread, it would not be strong enough to hold." Thomasse stepped to the fire and stirred the kettle. "I guess this means there is no fish in our stew tonight."

The vein in his temple ticked. "God's teeth, woman. Did I not just explain why?"

She flinched at the frustration in his voice. Retrieving the bowls from the sideboard, she scraped out the remains from the kettle. Tomorrow she would visit the manor cookhouse again and ask for more victuals.

"Maybe James can help," she said softly. "Perchance he has something in the stable with which to mend it."

Her father grunted and shoveled down the last of his stew. "I will go, but I do not approve of how much time you spend with that man."

He rose and hoisted the net onto his shoulder. "Bar the door, and do not open it for anyone but me." With that, he disappeared into the darkness.

With the horses bedded down for the night, James settled onto the pile of hay beneath the hanging lantern, and pulled out the block of wood and small knife from his pouch. He resumed whittling the toy horse. All the while, his thoughts centered on Thomasse, hoping she showed up for work on the morrow. It had taken a lot of convincing for his mother to agree to take her back.

Honestly, he did not know why he had bothered. Some misguided sympathy, perhaps, for someone who considered herself better than the common folk. Her kind might possess power and wealth, but underneath it all, they were no different—save for the happenstance of their birth or a bit of good fortune. Perhaps it was pity. But that did not explain why he eagerly anticipated their next meeting.

The stable door creaked. James jumped up, dropping the toy horse and knife, and grabbed a pitchfork. "Who goes there?"

A shadow slipped in through the door and stepped into the circle of light. "Whoa, James, it is I, Nicholas."

James lowered the pitchfork and returned it to its place against the wall. "To what do I owe the honor of this late-night visit?"

Nicholas lifted the fishing net from his shoulder. "It has a hole. Thomasse thought you might have something I could use to mend it."

The corner of James's mouth ticked. "I admire her faith, however, I am not capable of miracles."

Nicholas rolled his eyes. "Why did I listen to that girl? What would a groom know of fishing nets?"

"My grandfather was a fisher, so I know a little. Since you are here, let us take a look," James replied.

Spreading the net out on the ground, the two men examined it. Near the center a few of the fibers of the mesh were broken, leaving a hole big enough for most fish to escape.

"Any thoughts on a fix?" Nicholas asked.

"I do not have the proper materials for a repair, but we could braid together some hay for a temporary fix."

James quickly braided together several hay stalks and tied them together to mend the hole. "Mind, this will not hold long. You need to visit the market in St. Helier forthwith to purchase some flax twine." He handed back the net. "When you arrived, I had thought your sojourn would be but a few days. How long do you intend to stay?"

Nicholas shook his head. "I cannot speak to the duration. Things have not gone as I had planned."

"As the cottage has sat abandoned, you may stay as long as needed," James replied.

"Thank you for that," Nicholas said. "Before I go, there is another subject I wish to discuss."

James picked up the wooden horse carving and settled back onto the pile of hay, waiting for Nicholas to continue.

"I wish to speak of my daughter and your intentions."

"I have none."

"Let us be honest. A man does not spend so much time with a maiden without some intent, whether for good or ill."

"Surely you have noticed the soldiers about the isle. I accompany your daughter for her protection. That is all."

Nicholas relaxed. "I pray you speak truly. Once we return to England, she is to be espoused to a man of noble birth."

"Then you should be gratified to know I have vowed not to marry again. I have found contentment in caring for the horses. I need nothing more."

Nicholas slung the net onto his shoulder. "Thank you again for your help. I shall set out for St. Helier on the morrow to get proper twine."

The stable door creaked shut, and James stared at it for several minutes. Just another man with an elevated opinion of himself. But if Nicholas thought his warning would scare James away from his daughter, he was wrong. She needed protection. But even as he wanted to attribute his actions as noble, there was something more, he was just not sure what.

# Chapter Eight

The next day, before the other spinsters arrived, Thomasse presented at Colette's cottage. The woman nodded her approval as Thomasse retrieved her spindle and distaff. Colette used the time to demonstrate how to properly hold the distaff and let the spindle drop and spin.

When the day was finished, Thomasse was disappointed it was not James who accompanied her on the walk home, but rather a peasant boy. She arrived home to an empty cottage, her father having gone to St. Helier to buy twine for the fishing net; he would not return until the morrow.

Eating supper and going to bed alone was a new experience. Maybe she was not as tired, or maybe it was the solitude, but for the first time since their arrival, she was aware of the activity of the night beyond the cottage walls—not just the crash of the waves, but also the boisterous voices of French soldiers as they patrolled the shores, and the smell of roasting meat. The latter two made her uneasy, but eventually sleep came.

When her father returned late the next day, he brought no good tidings, only the twine. He had inquired of a French soldier in St. Helier about the arrival of the English royal family, only to be told there was no expectation of their coming. And thus, at present, there was no foreseeable end to their stay on Jersey.

With each passing day, her spinning improved. Her efforts regained her a modicum of respect, and with it a confidence that had not existed before. And the day Colette placed a few coins in her hand in payment for her work, Thomasse felt a deep sense of pride. In the market, she shopped for vegetables and bread, and treated herself to a small vial of jasmine oil. Rubbing it on her wrists made her feel as if something of her former self still remained.

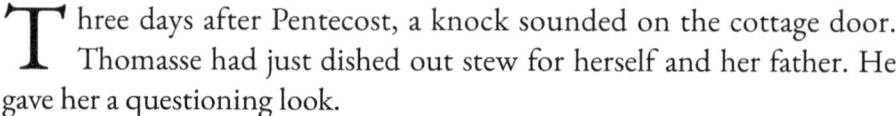

Three days after Pentecost, a knock sounded on the cottage door. Thomasse had just dished out stew for herself and her father. He gave her a questioning look.

She shrugged. "I am not expecting visitors."

Pushing back his chair, her father stepped over and unbarred the door, opening it a crack.

"Might I come in?" a male voice said.

Her father's back stiffened, but he opened the door and admitted the man. She recognized him as Seigneur de Carteret of St. Ouen's Manor. A look of terror flickered across her father's face before he schooled his countenance. He had dreaded this day would come—always fearful of being discovered and sent back to England in chains.

"My apologies for intruding upon your supper, but I want to speak with all those living on my manor personally," de Carteret said.

Her father pulled out a chair. "Pray, be seated."

The three of them gathered around the table. Thomasse and her father waited silently for the seigneur to say his piece.

"There are reports among the villeins," de Carteret began, "that the French garrison has become emboldened, extorting tribute from merchants and beating those who cannot pay. Menfolk in other parishes have been kidnapped and held for ransom in the dungeon at Mont Orgueil."

He paused, glancing briefly at each of them before he continued. "Some soldiers have forced fathers to watch as they foully used their daughters."

Thomasse's body shook, even as her mind struggled to comprehend how one human could be so cruel to another.

Her father gasped. "Can anything be done to curb them?"

The seigneur shook his head. "I have spoken with the captain of the garrison, but he sets no store by our protestations. Alas, as an occupied isle, we are at their mercy. The best I can do is advise our citizens to keep their heads down and avoid the soldiers."

"I appreciate the warning," her father replied.

"As foreigners, it would be better for you and your daughter to return home."

Her father looked away. "Regrettably, that is not possible."

The seigneur raised his eyebrows. "Indeed. If money is the obstacle, I have no problem providing funds for passage back to England." His eyes searched her father's face. "Surely nothing is more important than the safety of your child."

His gaze lingered on her father, who squirmed in his chair.

"We are content living here, are we not, Thomasse?" His eyes widened, and he kicked her beneath the table.

Thomasse forced a smile. "We would be happy to remain here forever."

Her father inclined his head. "I hope you will allow us to stay in this cottage."

The seigneur rose and strode to the door. "As the cottage was abandoned, you may stay—so long as you cause no trouble."

Her father scrambled up from his chair and bowed. "No trouble. No trouble whatsoever. We are grateful for your goodwill toward us."

The seigneur quit the cottage, and they watched as he climbed the hillock leading to the manor house. When he was out of sight, her father slumped into the chair.

"I think we are safe. Word of what I did must not have reached him. Or, by some good fortune, he does not recall meeting me in London."

"But Father, did you not say these soldiers are under the command of Queen Margaret's cousin? If so, can you not appeal to the captain of the garrison? Such brutality is intolerable."

"I am but one man, unknown to them. Like everyone else, we must avoid attracting their attention."

W alking home from the village, James and Thomasse passed fields of freshly cut rye. The summer harvest always caused her thoughts to linger on her mother and brother, now three years gone.

She had often poured out her sorrow to Agnes, but knew nothing of how her father had dealt with the grief of losing his wife and son—other than becoming distant from his only living child. *How tragic that we have never spoken of our mutual loss.* Even if she broached the subject, she feared he would shut her out, unwilling to expose any hint of weakness before his daughter.

"James," Thomasse said, timidly, "tell me about your wife."

James gazed into the distance. "Becca was my first love—the love of my life. We were best friends even in childhood." His voice was strained, cracking as he spoke. "She died giving birth to our first child." He paused as he composed himself. "Two Michaelmas have passed since. I have learned to accept it."

"I give you my compassion. You are still young. I hope one day you will find someone new to love."

"A love like ours is rare. One cannot expect to be so lucky a second time." James sighed. "'Twould be unfair to a new wife if she could never measure up. I am content to remain a widower."

She pondered his words. "Why do you never meet me at Colette's cottage?"

"For your sake, and mine."

"My sake?"

"People talk. I would not wish false rumors to spread that we have formed an attachment." There was a twinge of sadness at his words.

"Why must people make more of something than it rightly is?"

"I suppose it gives them something to gossip about." James grinned, his amber eyes twinkled. "However, I value our friendship."

"Indeed, I am grateful to have someone with whom I can speak freely." Thomasse stooped and gathered a few yellow wildflowers growing alongside the path and buried her nose in the blooms.

"Our conversations always lift my spirits," James said.

Thomasse slipped a hand through his arm. "After everything you have done for me and my father, I am grateful I can do something for you."

They continued the walk toward St. Ouen's Manor in silence, Thomasse saddened that such a kind man had determined to close himself off from love.

J ames strode toward the manor house, marveling at the change he had witnessed in Thomasse. When they first met, she had cared only for her clothes and returning to her privileged life in England.

She had gone from an entitled maiden to more than just a responsible woman—she had become sensitive to the feelings of others.

Pushing open the door, he entered the great hall, a cavernous room built of brown stone. A fire blazed on the hearth, and the room teemed with people. French soldiers and men-at-arms talked loudly as they supped.

Tonight, he could not face the noise and boisterous laughter. Filling a trencher, he returned to the stable to eat.

He settled onto a pile of hay, content with the company of the horses that snorted and nickered in their stalls. A hint of jasmine lingered in the fabric of his tunic. He tried to imagine Becca beside him. Instead, he saw Thomasse's sparkling blue eyes and brilliant smile.

# Chapter Nine

Yuletide brought twelve days of blessed relief from toil, and an open invitation to dine at the manor house on Christmas and Twelfth Night. A year ago, Thomasse had sat on the dais with her father dining on fine dishes. This year, they ate with the peasants and shared their humble fare. Another reminder of how much their lives had changed.

The winter days passed in quiet routine, each day much like the last. It was a fortnight prior to Ash Wednesday when her father declared the fishing sparse and the waters dangerous. He would sojourn to Mont Orgueil in hopes of receiving tidings of King Henry and the royal family.

He left with scant thought for Thomasse's safety. Keeping the door securely barred did not dispel her fear whenever loud male voices sounded beyond the door as the French soldiers patrolled the shores. Nor the anger that rose when the smell of roasting mutton wafted through the shutters—another sheep stolen from a poor tenant farmer. And each night, she prayed for her father's safe return.

He had now been gone thirteen days, and she had never known such loneliness. Her work and an occasional chat with James were the only distractions during her father's absence.

She wrapped her cloak tightly around her to stave off the February chill as she meandered through the village street. As she rounded the curve, she was surprised to see James waiting for her by the well. He greeted her warmly. "There is a betrothal celebration tonight. Would you care to join us?"

With her days spent laboring and her nights alone, she yearned for a bit of mirth. What harm could come of it?

She smiled. "That would be lovely."

They veered onto the byway leading toward the tenant farms. Children bounded out from behind a cottage, shrieking with delight, oblivious to the cold, and chasing a black-haired dog that kept just out of their reach.

The sounds of the celebration could be heard before they reached the cottage. Inside, the guests milled about. Mothers chatted with babes on their hips, while tots sat on their fathers' shoulders. The espoused couple, sat in the middle, the maiden's cheeks flushed, as guests shouted ribald comments—"Keep her warm, ye swain. Cold wife, cold cock"—"Keep yer manyard stiff till her belly starts a-swellin'."

Thomasse gawked. Never had she attended a celebration quite like this. In her younger years, she had been relegated to the nursery, forbidden to join in the fun. As a young lady, she had been instructed in proper behavior, acceptable subjects for polite conversation, good table manners, and admonished to always maintain her dignity.

As the sun set, the cottage darkened, and instruments magically appeared. The guests took turns singing and dancing. Even the children joined in the fun.

Thomasse stood next to the wall as she watched. At the parties she had attended in England, every guest had been adorned in their finery, so self-important. And while there had been laughter, it felt polite rather than joyous.

Even the dancing was different. She was accustomed to promenades, where guests preened like peacocks, eager to be admired. But tonight's dancing was all hand clapping and foot stomping—energetic and fun, accompanied by smiles and sincere laughter.

James interrupted her musings. "Shall we dance?"

She nodded eagerly. They joined the circle, moving right to left and back again, as she tried to mimic their movements. And when she moved the wrong direction and kicked when she should have clapped, no one seemed to mind. Just a bit of mirth, along with encouragement that she would soon get it right.

When the dance was finished, she collapsed on the ground with the others, overcome in gales of laughter.

The thunder of hooves silenced the merriment. Soldiers! The guests hushed, praying they would ride past, but a knock sounded on the door.

The host cracked it open and six soldiers shoved their way inside, swords drawn. They brandished their weapons in the faces of frightened women and children, barking out orders in French. "Gatherings are forbidden. Go home or be arrested."

The host pointed to the door. "Get out! You have no right to enter my home."

A soldier grabbed him, twisting his arm behind his back. Everyone gasped when they heard a crack and the host screamed in pain.

The soldiers laughed. "Serves him right for defying us," one said in French. "Make an example of him. Hang him outside on the tree."

Two soldiers shoved the host toward the door.

It was too much for Thomasse. She had stood by while these isle folk were punished for lacking the means to pay tribute—but to be terrorized for having a bit of fun? These people had done nothing wrong and did not deserve to be treated like criminals.

"*Arrête.* Stop," she yelled as she pushed her way through the guests. "*Ils ne veulent pas de mal.* They mean no harm."

A soldier wheeled about and pointed his sword at her breast. Her heart pounded, and her legs shook. What was she thinking? She might be brutalized and hanged for interfering.

The soldier leered at her, slowly licked his lips, then spoke to the other soldiers, "What do you think? Should we let the Jersey dog go for a turn with the damsel?"

"Indeed! I can hear the wench moaning, begging for more already," another soldier replied, making sucking sounds with his lips. "Her honey, sweet on my tongue."

"How dare you speak to me thus?" Thomasse placed her hands on her hips. Where she continued to find the courage to speak, she could not comprehend. "Are you not here to hold the isle for King Henry? I am the daughter of a loyal knight."

"Think you are too noble for our ilk? Not tonight, ma chérie," a third soldier sneered.

"Sour as milk. *Cette garce* needs a proper ride," the first soldier said.

Another soldier shoved the host into the center of the cottage. "Nay, better to gut this one like a fish before he swings."

"Unless you wish to anger the true king of England, I demand you leave these people in peace."

The first soldier curled his lip in contempt. "Of course, your ladyship, but only if these scum return to their homes forthwith."

"As you wish." She appealed to James for help. "I hope you can convince everyone to leave."

James repeated the soldiers' demands, and the guests quickly dispersed into the night. The brewster stopped to squeeze Thomasse's arm and whispered "Gramercy."

The soldiers released the host, who fell to the floor, groaning. They stumped out of the cottage. The first soldier turned back. "Next time there will be no mercy."

Thomasse rushed to the host's side. "He needs someone to set his arm."

"It will have to wait," James said. "'Tis too dangerous to fetch a healer tonight."

Thomasse looked up and saw the man's family and the espoused couple huddled, their faces fraught with worry.

"Can I have your apron?" Thomasse asked the woman she thought was the host's wife. "I can make a sling to take some of the pressure off until the healer arrives."

Once the man's arm was tended to, he was carefully laid on his mat for the night. After receiving assurances that someone would fetch Madame de Beauvoir in the morning, Thomasse and James slipped out of the cottage. She closed her eyes and offered a silent prayer of gratitude that the situation had resolved peacefully and without serious injury. Her knees buckled, and she felt herself falling.

James caught Thomasse as she collapsed. She turned in his arms and rested her head on his shoulder. The scent of her jasmine perfume, mixed with the relief that she was safe, made him momentarily forget everything else. Her body trembled, and the sudden, overwhelming desire to kiss her took him by surprise. But he had no right. Despite her current misfortune, she had been born a lady above his station. And nigh betrothed according to her father, although he had seen no sign of its verity.

A soldier shouted, and he whispered, "We need to get out of here."

Gripping her arm tightly, they hastened away from the cottage, retracing their steps along the byway from which they had come. Once out of sight of the soldiers, he said, "That was very brave. Without your intervention, someone may have died or been imprisoned tonight."

Her blue eyes met his, her voice breathy. "I have never been more frightened." She dropped her gaze. "Well, except for when you drew me out of the water."

"A most fortunate rescue." Something she had said to the soldiers nagged him. "Is it true your father is one of King Henry's knights?"

She bit her lip. "I merely said what I thought advantageous in the moment." The tremor in her voice hinted that she might not be telling the entire truth.

"Where is your father? He has been gone for some time. Should the seigneur organize a search party?"

Her eyes darted from side-to-side. "It has been but a few days. I am certain he will return soon, when he completes his business."

"Business? What business could a fisher have that requires such a lengthy absence?"

"He heard a name spoken, someone he had met previously," Thomasse said, avoiding his gaze. "He hopes they might help speed our return to England."

He watched her face closely. "And left his daughter unprotected?"

Thomasse pushed her braid behind her shoulder. "It was impossible for me to go. I promised your mother—"

"'Tis dangerous for a woman alone, particularly now you have drawn the attention of the soldiers. Stay with my family tonight."

Thomasse straightened. "I can care for myself."

He touched her arm, and it was like something sparked. He searched her face, wondering if she felt it too. "But if the soldiers show up at your cottage—"

"The door will be barred."

"You think a barred door will keep them out? One woman against several determined soldiers is hardly a fair fight."

She looked down the path leading to St. Ouen's Manor. "If you think it best. I suppose one night will not matter."

James tucked her arm through his as they walked back to the village, troubled by the feelings awakened by this woman.

J ames pushed open the door to his mother's cottage and beckoned for Thomasse to follow him inside. Colette and several children sat around the fire. All were quiet, probably still shaken by the night's events. In unison, they looked up, staring at her and James.

"I brought Thomasse here. I think it unsafe for her to return home to an empty cottage tonight," James said.

"Of course, she must stay," said Colette. "And you too, James. During these times, 'tis not safe for anyone after dark."

He retrieved mats and blankets for Thomasse and himself. She lay down and wrapped the blanket around her. She closed her eyes, but sleep did not come, her mind replaying the events of the evening over and over.

She rolled onto her side. James, already asleep, breathed deeply. His face was so much more handsome when devoid of worry. He had called her brave, and she thought he might kiss her. Would it have been gentle or fierce with passion? For some reason, she wanted to know.

Sleep finally descended, and she dreamed of lying amongst the flowers, the sun warm on her skin, her lover beside her, amber eyes filled with love.

She awoke, her body warm, damp with sweat, wishing the dream could linger. When she finally opened her eyes, James's mat was empty. She breathed a sigh of relief, certain if he had been there, her face would have revealed her secret.

# Chapter Ten

Thomasse hummed as she strolled through the village. It had been a marvelous day—so many folk had gone out of their way to thank her for the courage she had shown in standing up to the soldiers.

When she rounded the curve, James stood beneath the alder tree, hands behind his back, a mischievous twinkle in his eye. Her step faltered at the memory of last night's dream, thrilling, yet terrifying. James could not possibly know, but still, she felt shy, uncertain if he returned her regard.

James's arms swept forward, revealing a tussie-mussie of wild flowers. "'Tis not much—"

She took them and buried her nose in the blooms, breathing in their heady scent. "Oh, James, they are beautiful."

He cleared his throat. "A small token of our gratitude for last night."

They wandered down the path homeward, the conversation stilted as she turned over his words in her mind. He had said *our*, not *my*, gratitude. It would be presumptuous, perhaps too bold for a lady, to ask the meaning directly. Maybe he had chosen his words carefully, unsure if his attentions would be welcome. Still, she would not let her uncertainty dampen her happiness. There would be time enough to see where things went between them.

They parted at the crest of the hillock. Overflowing with joy, she skipped the rest of the way to the cottage, mindless of her dignity. She stopped short when she saw the door ajar. She slowly pushed it open, wary of what she might find inside.

Her father sat at the table. "Praise God, you are home safe."

She smiled brightly, dropped the flowers on the table, and kissed his cheek. "I could say the same about you. I have been so worried."

He did not return her smile. "Where have you been?"

"I have just come from my work in the village."

"Do not lie to me. I returned yesterday, eager to see my daughter, but you never came home last night. So I ask again, where were you?"

Her smile faltered. Rather than relieved she was safe, he was angry. She selected a chipped cup and filled it with water from the bucket. "I stayed in the village."

His piercing glare never wavered. "We are not so wealthy you can frivolously waste money on a room at the inn."

She set the cup on the table and arranged the flowers. "I stayed with a friend."

His eyes narrowed. "And does this friend have a name?"

Her jaw tightened. How dare he question her decisions when he had been absent for nigh a fortnight?

He rose, kicked back the chair, and pressed his fists against the table. "Were you with that groom? Tell me, did he take advantage of you?"

The last remnants of happiness drained from her body. "Of course not. How could you think thus?"

"How am I to think otherwise when you arrive home, humming, your hands full of flowers?"

"That I am happy. Given our changed circumstances, be grateful I have something to sing about."

He closed the distance between them, his nose in her face. "Were you or were you not with James last night?"

She narrowed her eyes and glared back at him, then stepped back and crossed her arms, refusing to be cowed. She had done nothing wrong. "Yes, but—"

"Fie, what shall I do?" He snatched off his hat and threw it on the floor. "You may have ruined more than just yourself. If Lord Jack finds out, he will withdraw his offer. Your union is the key to restoring our respectability and securing your future."

"How dare you slander my reputation." Her cheeks burned. "If you allowed me to finish. Last night, soldiers roamed the parish. It was unsafe for me to be alone, so I stayed with his family. I am sorry if I worried you needlessly, but do not judge without all the facts."

61

"Nevertheless, I forbid you to see him again. Is that understood?"

She clenched her fists, unable to believe his demand. James had provided for them when they were in dire need, and shown them nothing but respect. How dare her father treat James with such disdain? But from the stony look on his face, she knew argument was futile.

He flung himself back into the chair. "Do not look so downcast. You will forget him as quickly as all the others."

She turned away and collected the vegetables for dinner, chopping them fiercely, trying to dispel her anger. She tossed them into the kettle and hung it over the hearth. Fortunately, her father had seen fit to stoke the fire, so she did not have to, although foraging for wood would have been a blessed reprieve from his foul mood.

When the vegetables were softened, she ladled up a bowl of stew and set it in front of him. Too upset to eat, she perched on the chair opposite. An awkward silence stretched between them. If the tension did not abate, she could not remain here another minute.

"This is ridiculous! How long will you punish me for something I did not do?"

Her father stared at her as if she were a petulant child. "Do you not understand? I agonized many hours over the evils that might have befallen you."

"Yet here I am, hale and hearty. Can we put this behind us? If not, I shall sleep elsewhere tonight." When he did not respond, Thomasse pushed back her chair and stood.

Her father grabbed her hand. "Do not go. Perhaps I become vexed too easily."

Still peeved, but hoping to soothe the tension by changing the subject, she dropped back into the chair and asked, "Was your sojourn successful?"

He took a spoonful of stew and chewed slowly. "Queen Margaret has gone to France to gather support to retake the throne."

"And King Henry?"

"Still in Scotland. Once I have enough money for passage, I will join her."

"And what of me?"

"It will be safer for you to remain here. You seem to be adapting." Her father nodded in approval. "I commend you. But when our circumstances change, you must never confess to working as a spinster."

"What of you, Father? Will you confess to engaging in the fishing trade?"

"There is no dishonor there. It is all in how you couch it." He shoveled another spoonful of stew into his mouth. "Gentlemen often fish for sport."

Thomasse rose and collected the bowl and spoon and slammed them into the bucket.

Thirteen days her father had been gone. Thirteen days in which she had risen before the sun rose and hiked into the village to work. Thirteen days she had collected firewood, hauled water, slept alone, unprotected. No small feat. Men could boast for years about their exploits in battle, while her efforts to ensure their survival were to be forgotten, a tale unworthy to be told.

## Chapter Eleven

Deeply wounded by her father's accusations, Thomasse tossed and turned on her thin mat. Her father lay beside her snoring, apparently unbothered by their exchange. He seemed blind to how his words had hurt her. She was doing the best she knew how.

She had yet to confess her nagging guilt. Why had she let his loyalty to King Henry slip?

When they first arrived, the common folk had held for King Henry, but as the French soldiers became more ruthless, their loyalty had waivered. Although they did not openly voice support for King Edward, she was privy to the whisperings. If her father was in such a temper over her staying with James's family, how would he react if he discovered her indiscretion?

When sleep finally came, it was restless. The next morning, when James met her atop the hillock, her agitation must have been apparent.

"Is something the matter?" he asked.

"Nothing of consequence," she replied. Some things just needed to remain within the family.

"You look as though you have not slept."

She shrugged as they started down the path to the village. "My father has returned."

"Ah," James replied. "I trust his business was successful."

"I have been thinking about our conversation—when you asked if my father was one of King Henry's knights."

"Oh, that—I had forgotten about it already."

"Truly?" She swallowed hard. Although uncomfortable with deceit, if James exposed the truth, she and her father may be at risk. Now her unfortunate attempt to clarify made it more likely he would remember.

If he let it slip to the wrong person— "I would not want false rumors to spread."

James halted. "I accepted your explanation. Besides, I am not one to engage in idle chatter."

Between the awkward exchange and the weight of her father's accusation, conversation dwindled. She quickened her step. The sooner she reached Colette's cottage, the sooner she could drown out her thoughts with work.

When they reached the village, James said, "Something has happened. Last night you were so happy and now—something is troubling you."

Tears pricked her eyes, and she bit her lip. Despite her efforts to remain silent, the words spilled out before she could stop them. "My father has forbidden me to see you." She gasped at her *faux pas*. "James, I am sorry. My father is wrong to demand this of me."

"He is right. 'Tis not appropriate for a widower of my age to spend so much time in the company of a maiden he does not intend to marry."

"Why? We have done nothing wrong."

"True, but after the celebration, people are talking."

"What do I care? We know the truth. I refuse to sacrifice our friendship."

"But is it worth angering your father?" James asked. "If he has his way, you will return to England soon. The distance will end our friendship anyway."

Thomasse looked away. "I suppose you are right."

He touched her arm. "Goodbye, Thomasse." She watched as he strode back toward St. Ouen's Manor, certain her heart would break into a thousand pieces.

He might be a lowly groom, but she had never had a better friend. And despite her father's assurances, she had accepted that returning to England would not happen any time soon—if ever.

J ames glanced over his shoulder. Thomasse had not moved, her gaze still upon him. She looked small and lonely. He wanted to run back, to reassure her everything would be all right, but he continued walking, determined not to break his resolve.

The pain of losing Becca had been grievous, and he dared not risk such heartache again. And yet, this daughter of the gentry had wriggled her way into his heart, stirring a longing—a desire for a second chance at love. He shook his head, as if he could dislodge such wayward thoughts. She had spoken of friendship, not of love. He would hold on to that.

There were moments when he thought she might want more. What foolishness to think someone like her would ever consider him. Better to walk away, content in the knowledge of her kind regard than cling to false hope.

Once she returned to England, life would continue as before. The horses had been his salvation after Becca's death; they would be again. Hands tight on the reins of his heart, he would not look back.

# Chapter Twelve

The scent of candle wax and incense filled the air as Thomasse and her father entered St. Ouen's Parish Church for Easter services. Settling onto a rear bench, she studied the lovely arches and the high peaked ceiling. But as the church filled, she took up watching the congregants.

During the refrain of the first hymn, she spied Colette with her children in the doorway. Her heart skipped a beat when she spotted James standing behind them. Her gaze followed him as he settled on a bench near the front.

Her heart ached as she realized how much she had missed their conversations. Although she had made a few friends in the village, none had the same amiable spirit. James had always made her feel valued, like she belonged. She resolved to renew the friendship despite her father's disapproval.

When the final hymn ended, they escaped the church. "Father, I wish to greet some friends. You need not wait for me."

"Do not be long," he replied, then strode off in the direction of the bay-side cottage.

After greeting a few acquaintances, Thomasse hid behind a tree to wait for James. When he drew near, she whispered his name.

His eyes lit up. "Thomasse, 'tis good to see you. How do you fare?"

She stepped closer. "I am well, but I miss you."

"But your father—"

"I am seventeen, almost eighteen. It is time I took control of my life." Her words surprised her, a bold declaration of her desire for independence. "I earn my keep. Should I not be allowed to choose my friends?"

His smile vanished. "'Tis one thing to stand up to soldiers, and another to defy your father. Harmony at home is a blessing."

"I care not what he says." Reveling in her newfound courage, she wondered how James would respond if she took another bold step. Would he reject her request? Or feel obligated to accept? "Walk me home."

"As you wish," James replied.

They walked along the water's edge. After some initial awkwardness, discourse came easily, as if their last conversation had never happened. James talked about the new foals born or expected soon. Thomasse shared amusing tales of the other spinsters and people in the village.

They stopped and stared out across St. Ouen's Bay. "It has been more than a year since you pulled me from these waters." She looked up at James, her heart beat so loudly she was certain he must hear it. She placed a hand on his arm, surprised by her own boldness. "I would have died but for you."

"Pleased to be of service."

"Is that all?" she asked.

Their eyes locked. He shook his head. The yearning of her heart surprised her, and she suspected he felt the same, but his sense of propriety, his consciousness of her birth status, might deter him from ever declaring himself. "Then do not push me aside." Her voice sounded husky and breathless.

He put his hands behind his back, and she worried she may have pressed him too far. Or maybe she had misinterpreted his response. "I must," he said in a strangled voice.

She placed a hand on his chest. "Why?"

"Because—I have nothing to offer you."

"I care not. You are enough."

For a moment, she thought he might turn away. But suddenly his arms were around her waist, drawing her close, his lips on hers, gentle and warm, yet passionate.

She wrapped her arms around his neck, cherishing the exploration of feelings they had kept hidden like a guilty secret. With the truth confessed, she wondered how she had ever thought loving him was beneath her. He treated her more like a lady than many titled gentlemen. He was not born into nobility, but in his own way, he was noble.

When they parted, a shyness overtook her. She looked at him through lowered lashes. "Does this mean we are betrothed?"

James lifted her chin and she gazed into his beautiful amber eyes, soft with love. He wrapped her hair around his finger. "If you will have me."

"With all my heart." She reached up and drew his head down until their lips met again, their bodies melding perfectly.

They wandered along the shore, her hand warm in his, sometimes talking about inconsequential things or just being silent, listening to the breaking of the waves and the call of the gulls, content just being together.

When they neared the cottage, Thomasse said, "I should go on alone." His face fell. She raised on her toes and kissed his cheek. "I am not ashamed of our love, but my father is a hard man. I want to break the news at the proper time."

He squeezed her hand. "Until tomorrow then."

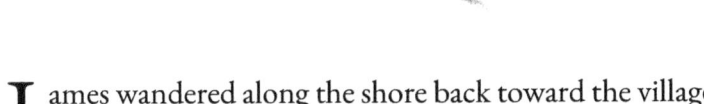

James wandered along the shore back toward the village, his mind spinning at the unexpected turn of events. He had awakened this morning with no thought of being betrothed before noon. Such good fortune that a woman as beautiful and kind as Thomasse had washed up onto the shore and into his arms. The Fates had surely played a hand.

Of course, this brought up serious difficulties. Where would they live? He had given up the bay-side cottage after Becca died, and living there with Thomasse's father was not an option he would accept. Nor could he ask her to sleep in the stable.

Self-doubt crept in. What if Nicholas convinced Thomasse to change her mind? And if he were not successful, he might take more extreme action. The same waters that had placed Thomasse in James's arms might separate them once again.

In the first flush of requited love, she may have considered him enough. Her father had spoken of her impending betrothal to a man of noble birth. Once she contemplated all the things she would need to forsake— the large estate, wealth and respectability, things James could never give her—would she still believe he was enough?

And then there was the seigneur. He must grant them permission—and then he must pay the bride price. James's heart clenched at the memory of the last time, when he and Becca had stood before the seigneur convinced their love could conquer any challenge. His whole world had been shattered by her death, her life cut short by the very consequence of marriage. Love had not been enough to spare her life.

His chest tightened. How quickly his heart had betrayed him. He stared out at the waves, remembering his past heartache, foolishly forgotten in a moment of desire. If history repeated with Thomasse, he feared he might not recover.

## Chapter Thirteen

When Thomasse reached the bay-side cottage, her father stood waiting outside the door. "I trust you had a pleasant visit with your friends."

"Delightful," Thomasse replied as they stepped inside. "Jersey is such a lovely isle. I would be content to call this place home."

"Nonsense," her father said as he settled into a chair at the table. "My daughter was meant for better things than being a spinster. I have not forgotten your love of beautiful gowns, parties, and the court gossip."

"God's bones, Father. This has been our lot for over a year." She retrieved cups and poured them each a draught of ale. "Edward still sits on the throne with no prospects of King Henry's return. Is it not time to abandon the delusion that we will return to our previous life?"

Her father wagged his finger. "Your ignorance shows. Raising funds and building an army in exile takes time."

Thomasse fetched vegetables and a knife. "For your sake, I hope you are right."

She sang as she chopped and dropped them into the bubbling kettle, her mind consumed with her newfound love with James. What would Eleanor and Maud think if they knew of her fondness for a groom with brown hair and amber eyes? She suspected Agnes would be conflicted, disapproving that James was of a lower station, but approving that he respected her.

When supper was ready, she scooped stew into bowls and placed them on the table, her heart light, unable to stop smiling.

"You are quite cheerful this evening. What has so elevated your mood?"

Thomasse sat, arranging her skirt, a bit self-conscious. "Nothing really other than Lent is over. No need to practice self-denial any longer."

Her father grunted in agreement. Hopefully soon, the perfect moment would present when she could tell him she had fallen in love with her noble groom.

Thomasse twisted and dropped the spindle. The day seemed agonizingly long, her thoughts constantly straying to James. When the bells tolled, she quickly stuffed the spindle and distaff into her basket of wool, not wasting a moment in polite chatter with the other spinsters. She wanted to run through the village into the arms of her beloved, but she dared not lest she make a spectacle of herself. Despite her lowered status, her mother's training in the proper behavior for a lady remained intact.

When she rounded the curve, James waited beneath the alder tree, a wide grin on his face. She lifted her skirt and ran to him. He grabbed her around the waist and swung her around. His long, lusty kiss took her breath away.

"I brought you something." He withdrew an apple from his pouch and handed it to her.

"Where did you find that?"

"A few remain in the cellar at the manor."

They settled onto the grass beneath the tree. She bit into the apple and chewed slowly, savoring the sweetness. "I could become accustom to your attentions."

James licked the juice from a spot on her lip. "I look forward to caring for my comely bride." He turned pensive. "Perchance we should not build our hope too high until we have your father's blessing and the seigneur's permission to wed."

She entwined her fingers with his and pushed out her bottom lip. "Why must we wait? Let us declare ourselves married and face the consequences together."

"We could, but I want to do things properly. I would not wish to claim your virtue and then have our marriage torn asunder by those with the power to do so."

Thomasse looked down at the apple core she still held in her hands. "I had not considered that." She tossed it aside and scrambled up. "Come, let us not think of that right now." As they walked, they held hands and spoke of their dreams for the future. At the crest of the hillock, Thomasse said, "Until tomorrow."

James kissed her hand. "Until then, my thoughts will only be of you."

James and Thomasse reveled in their blissful world. He often brought her small gifts; fruit, flowers, even a cross necklace he had carved from wood. She wore it tucked beneath her kirtle, the smoothness against her skin a constant reminder of his regard. The only thing marring their happiness was she had not broken the news to her father.

The wild orchids were in full bloom on a glorious day in May when James said, "I have a special surprise for you."

"Do I need to close my eyes?"

"Not at all," he said. "The seigneur seeks a tutor for his son. I spoke with him today, and he requests an audience in the morn."

She gasped. Had she heard him right? That she could have such an opportunity hardly seemed possible. "Truly? The seigneur would consider me—a woman?"

"With the French occupying the isle, it has proven impossible to hire an Englishman. It pains him to see his son's education suffer. I told him of your background—"

"But I have no experience—what if I fail?"

"Such foolish talk." James placed a light kiss on her mouth. "I have faith in you."

# Chapter Fourteen

Thomasse studied her palms, no longer the soft hands of a young lady of the gentry, but the rough, calloused ones of a peasant woman. The seigneur might question her capabilities if he made such an observation. If she kept them carefully folded, maybe he would not notice.

She settled onto a hard bench beside the door inside the great hall. An older manor, the walls and floors were built of brown stone. Light filtered through the windows set in the thick walls. The room bustled with preparations for the noon meal. French soldiers and men-at-arms milled about while servants laid the master's table on the dais before the large hearth. Others pulled trestle tables away from the walls where the common folk and servants would dine.

She smoothed the skirt of her blue woolen cotehardie, the same one James had given her when they first arrived. Strange how over the past year she had come to accept such humble attire with nary a thought. However, at the prospect of meeting with the seigneur, she became painfully aware of the threadbare spots, patches, and stains that stubbornly refused to wash out. At least she had the brush from James and could arrange her hair so she did not look like a disheveled waif. Hopefully. If only she had a looking glass.

A few minutes later, a servant directed her to the study at the far end of the room. She knocked softly and a deep voice beckoned, "Come in."

The room was small and dim, nothing grand like her father's study had been. One tiny window let in a bit of light, and the candle on the table did little to improve the situation. The sideboard beneath the window had seen better days.

De Carteret sat at a table that passed for a desk, studying a ledger. He closed it when she entered and leaned back in his chair. "How can I help you?"

She curtsied. "James said you wished to see me about the position of tutor."

He gestured for her to sit in the high-backed wooden chair opposite.

She perched on the edge of the seat, carefully arranging her skirt to hide the patches.

"What is your name?"

"Thomasse."

The seigneur slid the ledger aside and rested his arms on the table. "James tells me you were educated in England."

She inclined her head. "Yes, I studied many years alongside my brother."

"What subjects?"

"I learned to read, write, cipher, a bit of science, and a lot of English history. Also, I speak French."

He steepled his fingers against his chin. "And how does a learned maiden come to be on Jersey?"

She clasped her hands in her lap. How much could she disclose without endangering herself or her father? Perchance he already knew the truth of their circumstances and who they were. He would be remiss if he had not thoroughly investigated two foreigners in the parish. Indeed, it was quite possible that he knew her father from earlier days. Most of the noblemen and the gentry of England and Jersey were acquainted. She determined honesty would be best. All would be lost if she were caught in a lie.

"My father was in service to King Henry. Being no friend to the House of York, he thought it best we flee when King Edward ascended the throne. We are most grateful you have allowed us to take refuge here."

"And have you come to terms with your diminished status?"

"I admit, it was difficult at first." She lifted her chin. "I have spent my time learning to cook—though I admit rather poorly—and to spin. I earn my keep." She hesitated, her gaze meeting his. "One thing I learned, life can change in a moment. You can rail against the injustice, but fretting changes nothing. We must adapt to survive."

"Such wisdom from someone so young."

"When a person lives through what I have, you grow up quickly."

De Carteret smiled warmly. "My son, Philippe, desperately needs a tutor. He is but ten years of age. Do you believe yourself capable of teaching his lessons?"

She leaned forward. "I do."

"Then you will not mind if I give you a test."

"Indeed, I welcome it."

"Tell me, Thomasse, are you a God-fearing woman?"

"I am."

De Carteret retrieved a large Holy Bible from the sideboard. It thumped when it hit the table. He flipped through the pages until he reached the Book of Proverbs. "Read this passage."

Her voice rang out clear and steady as she read:

> *"These six things doth the Lord hate;*
> *yea, seven are an abomination to Him:*
> *A proud look, a lying tongue, and hands that shed innocent*
> *blood, an heart that deviseth wicked imaginations, feet that be*
> *swift in running to mischief, a false witness that speaketh lies,*
> *and he that soweth discord among the brethren."*

When she finished, she glanced up expectantly.

"My deepest wish is for my son to grow up to be an honest, just, God-fearing man. Do you think you can do that?"

"I cannot make that promise, but I welcome the challenge."

"A fair answer. I shall grant you a few weeks' trial to determine if you will suit. Considering these difficult times, you may be the perfect person to teach my son."

"Gramercy, Seigneur," Thomasse replied. "I appreciate the opportunity. I hope I do not disappoint."

"Report in the morning. My wife, Demoiselle Penna, will introduce you to Philippe." De Carteret reopened the ledger. "You may show yourself out."

When she reached the door, he said, "One more thing—a maid will prepare a room for you here at the manor."

Thomasse curtsied and quit the room, eager to share her good fortune with James.

J ames leaned on the pitchfork, satisfied that the stalls had been mucked and fresh rushes laid. Nothing like hard work to make time pass faster. He glanced toward the manor. Thomasse should be there by now. Hopefully, she would impress the seigneur.

Returning the pitchfork to the corner, James selected a brush and pick. Magnar nickered as James approached his stall. Grooming the powerful black destrier was a favorite part of his job. He dipped his hand into the grain barrel and withdrew a fistful of oats. Approaching slowly so as not to spook the horse, he opened his palm and Magnar nibbled at the treat.

Stepping inside the stall, he made long strokes along the stallion's back with the brush. The repetition was comforting—over and over until the coat glistened. Lifting the hind foot, he picked out the particles of debris.

The rushes crunched; Magnar snorted. James caught the scent of jasmine, and his heartbeat quickened. Thomasse stood outside the stall looking more lovely than ever.

She smiled. "I got the position."

He dropped the pick and swept her into his arms, spinning her about in a joyful dance. "I never doubted you."

"How can I ever thank you?"

"Tell me again that you will be my wife."

"I will." She lifted her left hand. "I cannot wait until your ring is safely on my finger."

He drew her to him, and lifted her chin. "Let us seal it with a kiss. I cannot wait for our forever to begin."

The next morning when Thomasse arrived at the manor house, a servant led her upstairs to her new chamber—a room with a proper bed! The door clicked shut behind her. Alone, she set her meager belongings— which comprised of nothing more than the brush James had given her and a bottle of jasmine oil—on the dressing table. She settled into the chair, picked up the brush, and held it close to her heart.

She stared into the looking glass. Would Eleanor and Maud even recognize her? Her skin had browned, and she looked older, the girl she had once been had vanished. In her place was a governess responsible for educating the seigneur's son. And someday soon, a wife!

She rose and stepped to the wardrobe. The servant had said she would find a selection of garments there. The undercurrent in her tone suggested the worn blue cotehardie was not acceptable attire.

Within hung three cotehardies, two in gray and one in blue, and a linen kirtle. She selected a gray one and laid it on the bed. Not new, but it had no patches or threadbare spots. She changed, then returned to the dressing table to comb her hair. This manner of living felt pleasantly familiar, except for no Agnes to tend to her needs.

She had just finished braiding her hair when a knock sounded on the door. "Are you ready?"

"Coming." She glanced once more into the looking glass before crossing the room and opening the door.

A stern woman dressed in a drab brown gown stood without, smelling of orange and cloves. A white wimple covered her hair. A rosary and a pomander hung from her girdle, and she clutched a prayer book. She surveyed Thomasse who shifted uncomfortably under the scrutiny. "I am Demoiselle Penna."

She beckoned Thomasse to follow and led her to the room next to her chamber. Light spilled through a large window, and the dark-haired lad she had seen sword fighting when she first arrived sat at the table in the middle of the room, looking at a map. He looked up expectantly. Thomasse sensed he was as nervous as she was.

"Philippe," Penna said, "this is Thomasse. She will be your governess until we can engage someone more qualified."

Thomasse cringed. Penna's words made her feel small, insignificant, even unworthy. Would the boy, Philippe, treat her the same? She wondered if she had treated their servants thus? She straightened her shoulders, determined to prove the demoiselle wrong. She was capable and qualified.

Philippe gazed up at her with his innocent, deep blue eyes, an unruly lock of hair falling over his forehead. "Will you leave like all the others?"

Unable to determine what to make of his question, she replied, "I intend to stay as long as your mother and father allow."

"You are younger and prettier than the others," Philippe replied. "I hope we will be friends."

"I hope so too." Thomasse smiled. At least the son did not seem to have adopted his mother's stern, dismissive manner.

"His last tutor left more than a year ago. He has had several, but none stay. I pray Philippe does not cause any trouble," Penna said. "I shall leave the two of you to get acquainted."

Thomasse waited until Penna left the room, then sat in the chair beside Philippe. "How old are you?"

"Ten. I had a sister once, but she died."

She placed a hand over his. "I am sorry. Being an only child must be hard. My brother died a few years ago."

"Was he a knight?"

"No, he was not old enough."

Philippe pulled over the map and pointed to England. "Someday I will go to London and become a knight like my father."

"Well, I shall never be a knight nor a lady-in-waiting." She sighed and placed a hand on her brow. "Probably never even a damsel in distress."

"Well, should that happen, I will save you."

Thomasse laughed. "I think we shall be great friends. Do you want to know a secret?"

Philippe nodded.

"I have never been a governess before," she said in a hushed voice. "You must teach me how it is done."

"Does my father know?" he whispered back.

She nodded.

Philippe held out his hand. "Friends?"

Thomasse put her hand in his. "Friends."

The conversation turned to things more educational as Thomasse probed Philippe's knowledge on a variety of subjects. By the time the morning was over, Thomasse was exhausted.

Returning to her chamber, she flopped onto the bed—so much more comfortable than the thin mat on the cold dirt floor of the cottage.

She rose and wandered to the window, delighted to discover it looked out to the stable. Her heart tugged, certain that James was thinking of her too.

## Chapter Fifteen

Her role as governess kept Thomasse busy: planning lessons, teaching Philippe, and answering his endless questions for hours. When the work day was over, and her time was her own, she spent it with James when his duties allowed. They ate supper together at night and strolled down tree-lined lanes during the long summer evenings. Lessons were suspended during harvest as all hands were needed to cut and bundle the rye. But every moment was magical when they were together.

On All Saint's Day, torches lit the crowded great hall of St. Ouen's Manor. The feasting had scarcely begun when James rose from the bench. "Meet me in the stable," he whispered.

Her curiosity piqued, Thomasse squirmed on the bench, waiting a respectable amount of time before slipping out the door and hastening to the stable where James waited.

He slipped his arms around her waist and drew her into a kiss. She wrapped her arms about his neck and breathed in his scent of horses, the scratch of stubble on her cheek a reminder that their love was more than just a dream. She felt his passion rise and her body responded; the intensity making her knees go weak. James led her to the pile of hay, pulling her down beside him. "I have wonderful news."

"Do not keep me in suspense."

"I have saved the bride price. I shall speak with Seigneur de Carteret on the morrow and gain permission for us to marry."

Thomasse looked down at her hands, not sure how to reply.

"I thought my news would make you happy."

"I am. Truly James, I am happy." Her stomach twisted. She thought she would have more time. She had hoped to spare his feelings, knowing her father still clung to the hope of making a noble match.

The stable door creaked, and rushes rustled. Magnar snorted and pawed the ground.

James put a finger to his lips, and they both listened. No voices or footsteps followed. Soon Magnar settled down, and all was quiet again.

"Must have been the wind," James said. "Once the seigneur grants permission, the banns can be posted."

Thomasse picked up a blade of hay and began peeling it into tiny threads.

"You have not told your father yet, have you?" James asked. She could hear the hurt in his voice.

She shook her head. "I am sorry. The right time has not presented."

"Are you having second thoughts?"

"No, never that."

"I had hoped we might wed before Advent. To spend the holy days cherishing my beautiful wife—that would be the greatest gift of this Yuletide."

"I would love nothing more. At night, I think of little else."

"Advent begins in three weeks. You must tell him."

The rushes crackled, and they both went quiet, eyes wide as footsteps approached. James jumped up and grabbed a pitchfork as Thomasse's father rounded the corner of the last stall.

"Must tell me what?" her father demanded. When neither spoke, he continued, "Thomasse, did I not forbid you to see this man?"

She scrambled up from the pile, straightening her skirt, removing bits of hay from the folds and one from her hair. Lifting her chin, she slipped her hand through James's arm. "We are in love and intend to wed."

"What do you know of love? I know your fickle heart. This whim will pass just like all the others."

"James is not a whim!"

"I have indulged your little fancies long enough. This time you have gone too far. What honorable gentleman will take a fair lady soiled by a low-born knave?"

"James is honorable. I ask that you grant us your blessing."

"I have promised your hand to Lord Jack."

"And where is he? Two summers have passed, and he has not come for me. It is James who saved my life and watched over us since our arrival. That is more than can be said for Lord Jack."

"You speak of things you do not understand. As my daughter, your duty is to obey me." Her father grabbed her arm. "Come, I am taking you home."

Thomasse clung tighter to James's arm. "I am staying with James."

James disentangled Thomasse's arm from his. "Go with your father. We will work this through later, when he has calmed."

"That will make no difference," her father replied. "I will never give my blessing for the two of you to wed. Do not come near my daughter again."

Her father grabbed her arm and led her from the stable. Thomasse's face burned, furious at being treated like a naughty child rather than a grown woman who knew her own heart. Why did her father have to be so unreasonable? He refused to accept the truth that this life was their future.

How could she face James again after such humiliation? Even the seigneur's permission meant nothing without her father's consent.

# Chapter Sixteen

P rayer book and lantern in hand, Thomasse slipped into the chapel through the side door. The priest was in the midst of offering a prayer as she eased the door shut. She shuddered. Somehow, she had lost track of time. There would be no escaping the forthcoming rebuke. She tiptoed toward the front. The congregants' heads were bowed, and her breath caught when her gaze fell on James, seated on a back bench.

They had not spoken since that mortifying day. Too ashamed to face James, she had taken meals in her room. No amount of apologies could fix the hurt she had caused. That is unless she could convince her father to relent.

Thomasse and her father had parted ways in anger after the incident, and she hoped that, in the spirit of the holy days, they could set aside their differences and reconcile.

After vespers, she would ask Penna for permission to visit him. She would plead James's and her case, even though she knew her father was unlikely to relent.

Philippe caught her eye as she slid in beside him and set the lantern and prayer book beneath the bench. Penna, eyes closed in prayer, clasped her rosary. But it was the seigneur's absence that surprised her. He never missed vespers. And to be absent on Christmas Eve—

"In the name of the Father, the Son, and the Holy Ghost. Amen."

The congregation rose for the final hymn, and her spirit soared. When she sang, the cares and worries of life faded away. When the final refrain ended, the momentary lull broke into a hum of conversation.

"Is Father ill?" Philippe asked his mother.

Penna looked down her nose. "He is delayed on a matter of business."

Thomasse's heart squeezed. Philippe was only a lad worried about his father, and yet his mother dismissed his concerns.

Stern faced, Penna pushed past Philippe to confront Thomasse. "You arrived late to services."

Thomasse stared at her boots. Of all the nights to draw the woman's displeasure. "My apologies, Demoiselle Penna."

Her lips pinched into a thin line. "See it does not happen again. Seigneur de Carteret and I expect you to set a good example for Philippe."

"Yes, Demoiselle Penna." Thomasse took a deep breath. "With your permission, may I spend Christmas Eve with my father?"

Penna inclined her head. "Give him our Yuletide greetings."

"Gramercy. I shall return in the morning." Thomasse curtsied and collected her prayer book and the lantern from beneath the bench.

She shivered as she stepped out into the crisp night air. Lighting the lantern, she hastened down the path leading to the bay-side cottage. She lifted the lantern higher, spilling light across the path as it inclined.

Philippe's voice drifted through the night air. "Wait for me!" She halted until he caught up. Together, they trudged up the hillock and watched as the last bit of light vanished from the sky.

"It is cold. You should get home lest you become ill," Thomasse said.

"I wanted to wish you Happy Christmas."

"The same to you and your family."

With the tip of his right patten, Philippe drew circles in the mud. "Can you forgive my mother?" he mumbled.

"Do not blame her. I was the one in the wrong."

The bells of St. Ouen's Parish Church pealed, announcing the official end of Advent and the commencement of the Christmas holy days. In the distance, pinpoints of light danced as the villagers rushed home after vespers.

Philippe touched her arm. "Take care. Evil men lurk in the dark."

Thomasse's heart warmed, and she hugged Philippe. "You put too much stock in servants' tales. The cottage is just down the hill." She tousled his hair. "I promise to be back by morning."

She watched Philippe cross the green and disappear safely into the house. Lowering the lantern, she stepped cautiously as she navigated her way down the hill. It would not do to turn an ankle in the dark, for no one would miss her since this visit to her father was a surprise.

A sliver of moon slid out from behind the clouds, its reflection shimmering on the water. A ghost-like ship floated just beyond the bay. With its sail down, the mast looked like a dead man's hand reaching up from the depths. The hair on the back of her neck prickled. Heart pounding, she hastened to the cottage. When her knock went unanswered, she pushed the door open, stepped inside, and barred the door. She leaned against it, drawing several unsteady breaths. Philippe's warning must have sent her imagination reeling.

A few embers glowed on the hearth. She selected a couple of logs from the woodpile beside the door and stoked the fire, then settled onto a chair at the table to await her father's return.

James watched Thomasse quit the chapel. He made to follow, but was stopped several times by people offering Yuletide greetings. He lost sight of her, and by the time he stepped out into the cold evening air, she was not on the green. She must have hurried back to the manor house to avoid him.

He leaned against the outer wall of the chapel. So much for the extra care he had taken when combing his hair; she had not even glanced his way.

A light bobbed in the distance, moving along the path to the bay-side cottage. It could only be Thomasse. He sighed. He would not chase after her. If life had worked out differently, they would be walking home together, husband and wife. Instead, he must content himself with watching her from afar—the only way he could ensure that no harm befell her, at least as far as the crest of the hillock.

"Have you seen Thomasse?" Philippe asked.

James, startled from his reverie, kept his eyes on Thomasse. "What?"

"Never mind, I see her," Philippe said, and took off like a colt galloping down the path.

"Wait for me," Philippe called.

She stopped and waited until Philippe reached her, and they walked on together. *If only that were me,* James thought. How mad to envy an eleven-year-old boy.

Since the confrontation with her father in the stable, they had not spoken. He had searched for her in the great hall at meal times, but she did not show. At first he thought she needed time to work through her feelings. But as time passed, and she still did not show—well, he did not know what she thought. Did she resent him for not pleading harder for her father's blessing? Though he regretted it now, he doubted the outcome would have been different. Did she doubt the depths of his love? He hated that things had ended so badly—so many things left unsaid.

The bells of St. Ouen's Parish Church pealed in the distance. Philippe sprinted down the hillock, across the green and into the house. When James looked back, Thomasse had disappeared.

The sound of hooves in the darkness caught his attention. Geoffroi de Beauvoir, the manor's reeve, appeared. He sought out Penna, who paled as he spoke. Then he wheeled his horse and galloped off into the night.

Penna hastened over, breathless, her eyes wild. "Geoffroi has just brought word—there are pirates in the bay."

"Thomasse!"

"You need not worry. The bells of St. Ouen's Parish Church will sound the warning for all to flee to Grosnez Castle. Come, we must prepare the manor for attack."

The cry of the gulls pierced Thomasse's consciousness. She jerked backward, unsure of her whereabouts, until her gaze lit upon the fishing net hung neatly on the wall. She glanced around for her father, but she was alone; his mat showed no signs of being slept in. Her mind raced as she ticked through all the mishaps that may have befallen him.

Common sense soon prevailed. One of the tenant families must have invited him to dine, and he stayed the night. So much for her Christmas Eve surprise.

She busied herself as she awaited his return, stoking the fire and preparing a stew. With nothing left to fill the time, she retrieved a distaff and three spindles from the basket atop a small dresser between the bed mats. It had been months since she had last done any spinning, and she wondered if she still had the skill. She slipped two spindles into her pocket, grabbed a handful of wool, and settled next to the fire.

She had just started on the second spindle when her eyes stung and watered, and the cottage filled with the stench of scorched gravy and burnt cabbage. Setting aside the distaff and spindle, she threw open the shutters before grabbing the ladle and stirring the pot. Footsteps sounded outside. She dropped the ladle, eager to greet her father. She opened the door, coming face-to-face with a tall stranger. His bedraggled hair hung to his shoulders, his garments sodden, his scabbard awry.

She gasped. "Who are you?"

"Praise God. You speak English." His voice was a pleasant, deep baritone. "My ship capsized in the bay. I would be much obliged if you would invite me in to get dry."

Her first thought was to slam the door, send him away. But with circumstances similar to her own, how could she not pity him? She paused, uncertain. It would be rude not to extend the same favor James had when they first arrived. From the stranger's manner of speech, she perceived him to be an Englishman of some merit. Surely all would be well. Besides, her father would be along shortly.

She beckoned him inside, and he strode over to the fire, removed his cloak, and spread it on the ground. He reached out his hands to the warmth and his eyes lighted on the kettle. "I hesitate to impose further, but might you spare a bite to eat?"

"I am certain my father will not object," Thomasse replied. "I did not catch your name."

"Many pardons. The name is Hareford." He bowed deeply. "John Hareford, in service to the Earl of Warwick."

She startled at the title. If this man represented Richard Neville, he had probably come as a guest of Seigneur de Carteret, a fellow Yorkist, and she had done well not to cause offense.

Thomasse selected a bowl and ladled out a hearty portion of stew, then fetched a spoon, a tankard, a portion of bread, and a pitcher of ale, and placed them on the table.

"I regret I have nothing better to offer."

He plopped into a chair. With his foot, he pushed out the chair opposite and indicated she join him. Thomasse sat primly, hands clasped in her lap. She recoiled as he wolfed down the stew, smacking his lips. He poured himself a tankard of ale and requested another bowl of stew. Glad for something to occupy her hands, she complied.

When he had sopped up the last bit of gravy with the bread and downed the ale, he wiped his mouth on his sleeve and poured himself another tankard. "I hoped to speak with your father."

"Why? Do you know him?" Her legs felt weak, and she grabbed the chair to steady herself. Surely King Edward would not pursue them here.

"I imagine not," Hareford replied. "I wished to thank him for his hospitality." He scrutinized her face. "Have we met before?"

"Seems an impossibility."

"You neglected to tell me your name."

"Thomasse."

Hareford drained the contents of the tankard, then returned to the fire. Despite the warmth, he shivered uncontrollably.

"Let me fetch a blanket." Her nerves prickled as she felt the man's eyes track her every move, like a cat hunting its prey. *What is keeping Father?*

She handed him the blanket, and he wrapped it around his shoulders. When she saw the expression of gratitude in his almond-shaped blue eyes, she felt a twinge of guilt for thinking badly of him.

He continued to gaze at her. "You are a handsome maiden."

The silence stretched awkwardly. Finally, Hareford said, "Forgive me if I have been too forward. When do you expect your father?"

Thomasse shook her head. "Some unexpected delay. Perchance I should go search for him."

A laugh escaped his lips. "Perhaps you have sought to deceive me."

His words sounded casual, but the hair on her neck raised. Her chest tightened. She reached into her pocket and her fingers closed around the spindle. What had she been thinking, inviting a man into the cottage when she was alone? Even if nothing unseemly occurred, a maiden's reputation could be ruined. Her feet itched to flee, but they seemed rooted to the ground.

He let the blanket drop from his shoulders and moved toward the door.

She breathed a sigh of relief. Clearly, he was a gentleman and understood the impropriety of being alone with a maiden. She picked up his cloak and held it out. "Do not forget your cloak."

He did not turn back, but sauntered over and barred the door.

T homasse floated between wakefulness and darkness, conscious of pain in every part of her body. The left side of her face throbbed. Slowly, the haze faded and full awareness returned. She opened her eyes and struggled to sit. How had she come to be lying on the hard table, unable to move her legs? Looking down, she screamed at the sight of her torn kirtle and blood-streaked skirt.

Her pulse raced when she saw Hareford by the fire, dipping a torch into the flames. Memories of his unwelcome advances flooded in, and she struggled against her bonds. "Untie me!"

He leered, the gash on his left cheek a sign that the spindle had hit its mark. "Had you cooperated, it would have been unnecessary."

He lifted the torch from the fire and touched it to the dry rushes.

The room spun as she struggled harder against the bonds. "What are you doing?" She could scarcely breathe. Surely, he did not mean to burn her alive.

He donned his cloak and strode to the door. "I cannot leave you to tell tales."

"You are a monster!"

He smirked as he lifted the latch. "Those feelings will be short-lived. By the time the fire consumes the cottage, you will bless me for not sending you to your maker a virgin."

"Please, I beg you. Do not leave me—"

He slipped out the door and pulled it shut behind him.

Her eyes watered and itched as smoke filled the cottage. Her fingers fumbled uselessly as she picked at the wool threads wrapped about her ankles. She uttered a quick prayer. "Dear God in Heaven, spare my life."

Outside, a dog barked and men shouted. *Could my prayer be answered already?* The door scraped along the dirt floor, and the shadowy figure of Philippe appeared. He coughed and waved his arms, then stepped back outside. A moment later, he reappeared, his cloak covering his mouth.

"Get low to the ground," she yelled.

Philippe crawled toward her and pulled a dagger from his pouch and sawed at the bindings.

"Give it to me." Her voice was edged with panic. "Smother the fire!" Philippe handed her the dagger, and she waved it toward the back of the cottage. "Grab the blanket!"

Philippe scanned the room. "I do not see one."

"In the back corner." She tried to sound calm, but her voice was shrill.

Her hands trembled as she attempted to cut away the bindings. Given the awkward angle, her efforts were futile. The flames licked along the rushes, moving closer to the cook fire. "Hurry!"

Philippe beat at the flames, his actions spurring their progress.

"Drop it on top."

He dropped the blanket over the flames. "Now what?"

Fearing the blanket might ignite, making the situation more precarious, she yelled, "The sideboard by the window! The bucket! Wet the blanket!"

He crept along the floor, feeling for the bucket. When he found it, he picked it up and sloshed the water over the blanket. The fire hissed like a snake as it died out.

Thomasse closed her eyes and slumped forward. The worst danger had passed.

"Let me help."

She opened her eyes and Philippe stood before her with an open palm, and she placed the dagger in it.

He quickly cut away the threads, and she tumbled off the table, throwing her arms around his neck, tears wetting her cheeks. "I prayed someone would find me."

She drew back, aware of the impropriety of her actions and the state of her clothing. She clutched the edges of her torn kirtle and leaned against the table. "I feel unwell." She clapped a hand over her mouth, the other over her stomach, and rushed toward the door, but her legs crumpled beneath her.

Philippe lifted her up, wrapping one of her arms around his neck, and put an arm about her waist, and steered her out the door. On the threshold, she heaved. When she finished, she leaned against the wall of the cottage, shivering.

Philippe ducked back inside. *I pray he does not understand what happened to me. He is too young.* From the other side of the cottage, she heard the voice of the seigneur, and a knot formed in her stomach. *If he suspects, my future as Philippe's governess may be over. And if my father turns me away, where will I go?*

The stranger's voice drifted from the other side of the cottage and that of a third man. *James.* She covered her face with her hands. *Why did it have to be James?*

Philippe returned with her cloak and draped it over her shoulders. "Who was that man?"

She shook her head. "I do not know. Some Englishman—said his name was John, that his ship capsized in the bay."

"Most likely a pirate," Philippe said. "Must have got left behind when the others fled to the ship."

"My father!" Thomasse gasped.

"He took shelter at Grosnez Castle with the other tenants and the sheep. He must be worried about you. I will send someone to let him know you are safe."

She stared ahead, seeing nothing, feeling nothing. So strange to feel completely numb, as if she was looking at herself from outside of her body. "My father must never know."

Philippe fetched his horse. "You need a leech. I shall take you to the manor house."

She grabbed his arm. "Philippe, promise you will not tell my father."

His face looked serious. "He will learn nothing from me."

He helped her into the saddle. Every movement was painful, but at least she would not have to walk.

When they reached the crest of the hillock, a dog barked. Thomasse looked toward the sound. The seigneur and James were astride horses, heading down the path to the village. The pirate, Hareford, stumbled along behind them, a rope tethered about his neck, his hands bound behind him, Puddles nipping at his heels. At least there would be some justice. She could take comfort knowing no other woman would suffer at his hands.

James kept the roan's pace slow as the pirate stumbled along behind on the way to the village. He would be held in the gaol until he could be turned over to the French.

It hurt that Thomasse avoided looking his way. But after the thoughts that had—and had not—crossed his mind earlier, he did not consider himself worthy of her attention.

When they learned that Thomasse was not at Grosnez Castle, it was Philippe who had pleaded for a search party. When he witnessed a man leaving the cottage, his heart nigh broke, believing that she had entertained some swain alone. But when the hound bounded down the hill and the man raised a burning torch, the truth had crashed over him, and his heart gripped with fear. He wanted to race his horse down the hillock and rescue her, but the seigneur had given that responsibility to Philippe, while he and the seigneur apprehended the pirate.

He had watched as Philippe led the gelding, with Thomasse seated atop, up the hillock toward the manor house. She had turned and looked his way, and his stomach had dropped at the sight of her swollen face, marred by bruises, and torn clothes.

He glanced back at the pirate, noting the fresh gash on the man's left cheek. She had fought him, engaging in a fight she could not win. His jaw clenched as he struggled to quell the storm rising in his chest.

And the guilt. This was his doing. If he had stood up to her father, they might have been married now, and this would not have happened. Rather than being there to comfort her, to assure her one day she would know joy again, he must content himself in aiding with the imprisonment of the vile man who hurt his beloved Thomasse.

Thomasse groaned as Madame de Beauvoir poked and prodded while Penna looked on. Everything hurt. She flinched when the healer touched the bruise where the pirate had struck her. She refused to think his name, for he deserved nothing more than her hatred. Strangely, the pain of her outward wounds paled in comparison to the torment that rent her soul.

Madame pulled the kirtle down over Thomasse's knees. "Your injuries are severe. They will heal, but the damage may leave you barren." She rummaged through her satchel of medicines and produced a bottle. "To ensure no long-term consequences, drink this elixir, a dose each day until it is gone." She set it on the dressing table, then gathered her satchel. "I will return in a few days to check your progress."

"Thank you, Madame de Beauvoir," Penna said. "I will personally ensure Thomasse takes the draught."

Thomasse rolled away, not wanting the women to see the tears that streamed down her face. She dared not speak lest she dissolve into sobs. This was her fault. If she had listened to her instincts, she would have slammed the door in the stranger's face. But instead, she had invited him in. If only she had returned to the manor when she discovered her father was not there.

When Madame had gone, Penna perched on the edge of the bed, her expression filled with pity. "No need to pretend. I may not be your mother, but I can hold you while you cry."

Thomasse sat, and Penna wrapped her arms around her. The tears flowed like a broken cistern. *Would they ever cease?* But finally, the well ran dry. Thomasse drew away, and Penna produced a kerchief from her pocket.

Thomasse sniffed. "Thank you for your compassion."

"In this moment, I saw my dear, sweet daughter. If she lived, and I were gone—" Penna's voice trailed off. "Get some rest. It helps the body heal."

As Penna rose to leave, Thomasse grabbed her sleeve. "Pray, do not tell my father."

"I will keep your secret and request the seigneur do likewise." She glided toward the door. "However, I can make no promises on his behalf."

Thomasse's heart swelled with gratitude. A human heart hid beneath Penna's stern façade. But she knew better than to trust the lady's benevolence to last long.

## Chapter Seventeen

Penna's benevolence lasted through the Christmas holy days, but with the arrival of Epiphany came the summons—Thomasse was ordered to attend the celebrations. The house blessing had proved difficult. The music and singing harkened to happier times, and she escaped to the safety of her chamber immediately after.

Staring into the looking glass above the dressing table, she gently fingered her cheek, no longer black and blue, but a sickly yellowish green. At least the swelling had subsided. Soon, she would appear whole again—at least on the outside. But how long until the inner wounds healed?

Now she had to gather what remaining strength she had to endure the midday feast. An open invitation had been issued to the entire parish, and her father would probably attend. She would now have to face him—and James. Having been confined to her chamber for many days at Madame de Beauvoir's instruction, she had seen neither of them since that day. Would her father guess the truth?

She slipped on her shoes and trudged down to the great hall. Her heart sank when she spotted James at the bottom of the stairs. She closed her eyes. *What must he think of me? Does he blame me for what happened?*

She could not bear it if he looked at her with disdain—perhaps all he saw now was a ruined maiden.

Every part of her longed to run back to her chamber, lock the door, and hide beneath the blanket. Unfortunately, that was not a possibility.

She opened her eyes and drew a deep breath before descending the stairs.

James smiled hesitantly. "I thought to sit with you," he said. "No need to talk. Sometimes 'tis nice to just have a friend close by."

Tears welled in her eyes as she descended the last steps, grateful James somehow understood. If her father were present, having James beside her, no matter how much he disapproved, would give her courage.

James offered his arm and led her across the great hall.

Her father stood in the far corner, his body thinner, his hair limp beneath his worn hat. His eyes widened as they approached. "Thomasse, what happened?"

She avoided his gaze. "I came to visit you Christmas Eve and stumbled over a chair in the dark." She held her breath, wondering if he would perceive the lie.

"That explains the disorder I found upon my return. I thought maybe pirates ransacked it." He smiled wryly. "Not that I have anything worth taking."

Her father scanned the great hall. The tension drained from her body, thankful he seemed too preoccupied to pursue the conversation further. He did not even seem to notice James beside her.

Her father leaned in close and whispered, "My ship leaves in the morn. I go to join Queen Margaret d'Anjou." He squeezed her hand. "Keep the faith. Ere long we shall return to England in triumph."

Her chin trembled. "But Father, what of me? I shall be all alone."

He glanced at the lord's table. "You are well taken care of here. I must take this chance to regain my title and lands."

She threw herself into her father's arms and hugged him tightly. "What if I never see you again?"

"Do not fret over things that may never happen." He returned her embrace, then pulled away. "I must be going. I just came to bid you farewell." He touched his hat and glared at James, but said nothing.

Thomasse watched as her father wove his way through the crowd until the door closed behind him.

James touched her back. "I see places in the back corner."

Once they had settled onto a bench at a trestle table, Thomasse said, "Strange my father did not ask more questions. The cottage was a horrible mess."

James leaned over and whispered in her ear. "Philippe told me you did not want your father to know. I cleaned up the cottage ahead of his return from Grosnez Castle."

She fumbled with the laces of her cotehardie. "After everything, you did that for me?"

"I could never wish you ill."

Servants filed in carrying platters of meats, fruits, nuts, bread, and cheeses. A trencher was placed before Thomasse. She picked at her food. Although it smelled delicious, she had no appetite.

She gazed about the room. Several women huddled near the side-board, whispering and glancing furtively in her direction. They turned away quickly when they saw her looking their way, and she wished she could shrink from sight.

James tensed. He mumbled something that sounded like, "I have a mind to tell those hens to keep their gossip out of the gutter."

Thomasse's face heated. "Please, do not think you need to defend my honor."

"You have endured enough without idle rumors."

She touched his arm. "Gramercy, but I do not deserve such kind-ness."

The Epiphany performances commenced with players enacting the scene of the Magi presenting gifts to the baby Jesus. In the past, she had enjoyed such entertainments. Now it felt like an obstacle, prolonging the feast, keeping her from the safety of her chamber.

When the performance ended, the room erupted with cheers. The chief baker entered carrying a platter holding the kings' cake, and set it before the seigneur.

De Carteret delivered a speech and a small, dark-haired lad tottered forward, followed by a young maiden dressed in a green gown, a babe on her hip. Much commotion ensued, culminating in the maiden holding a tray of cake slices as the lad scampered about the room, handing them out to the guests.

A cold breeze hit Thomasse's back when the outer door opened and slammed shut. The room hushed as every eye turned toward the newcom-er. A disheveled young man, his face red and puffy, staggered across the room and leaned against the lord's table, arguing with someone. Whispers rippled through the crowd—"'Tis the Bastard of Rozel."

The sot pointed at the maiden in the green gown, who stood rooted in the middle of the room, eyes wide. He lurched toward her, and she shrank back, drawing her charges closer. He circled behind her and placed a lingering kiss on her nape, his hand caressing her shoulder in a manner a bit too familiar.

Thomasse's stomach wrenched as a similar memory of the pirate surged in. She jumped up from the table, nearly tripping over the bench. She squeezed through the guests, tripping over her skirt as she stumbled up the stairs to her chamber. She leaned against the door, gasping for breath.

Unfortunately, the door was not thick enough to block out the shouts drifting up from below. She crawled away and leaned against the bed, covering her ears.

Below, the door slammed and more memories rushed in; the thump of the latch barring her escape from the bay-side cottage, that beastly man cornering her like a frightened animal, his warm breath on her neck, the sour stench of ale—

No. She would never think of it again.

Grabbing the bedpost, she placed one hand over the other as she drew herself to a stand. She lit the candle on the bedside table, noting the cup of elixir waiting for her. She padded across the cold stone floor to draw the heavy curtain, blocking out the sunlight.

In the dim light, the scene downstairs replayed in her head. Thomasse trembled as she recalled the man's drunken, erratic behavior, and the terrified look on the maiden's face when he kissed her neck.

Were all men like that? Her mind raced to other swains who had stolen kisses in the hidden corners of the garden. Had she just been lucky all those times?

Her head jerked up at the quiet tap on the door—most likely Penna come to make sure she drank the elixir. Picking up the cup, she emptied the contents into the chamber pot and crossed to the door.

"Who is there?"

"Philippe. You left early from dinner. Are you unwell?"

For the first time since Christmas day, her heart brightened, and she opened the door. "I am glad you have come. I never thanked you for saving my life."

"I was not permitted to see you," Philippe mumbled. "Mother and Madame de Beauvoir kept your door guarded."

Thomasse beckoned him to come in. She perched on the bed and patted a spot beside her. "Sit with me for a few minutes."

"You look better." He reached out to touch her cheek, and she flinched. "Did I do something wrong?"

"I am still nervous about being touched since—you know—" She lowered her head. "That day changed me."

"How?" He studied her face for a moment. "Your face might be bruised, but it will fade. You still look beautiful to me."

Thomasse wrung her hands. "Something inside has broken, and I do not know how to fix it." She took a deep breath and released it slowly. "I find it difficult to be in company, to witness the happiness of others, folks going on with their lives as before. And when they see me, they whisper." What she refrained from saying was that, despite her story, she feared they knew the truth, as if her sin and shame were branded on her forehead.

"I have told no one," he said.

She clasped both his hands and said, "Bless you, Philippe," then quickly released them.

He picked at the hem of the blanket. "And your father? What did you tell him?"

"That I tripped over a chair."

"You should be honest with him. He is worried about you."

"What makes you think that?"

"It is what father's do."

Those simple words of a child broke something new. The fact that she dared not—even feared—telling the one person she should be able to turn to for understanding and protection intensified her mental anguish.

Philippe searched her face, earnestness in his piercing blue eyes and that obstinate lock of hair falling over his forehead. "I would never hurt you like that bad man did."

Thomasse brushed the hair away from his eyes. "Of course you would not—you were the answer to my prayer."

Philippe slid off the bed and headed to the door. "I better go before Mother discovers me here."

"Philippe, remember to say your prayers."

He nodded, and the door clicked shut behind him. Thomasse laid down and pulled the blanket tightly around her.

Philippe's innocent words vexed her. For too long she had excused her father's indifference. She clenched her teeth, her body flushing with heat. Tonight, obsessed with his ambition, he had shown little concern for her well-being. It wasn't just his distraction that angered her, but every bad decision he had made that led to her downfall and disgrace.

If he had not hung Richard of York's head over the gate...

If he had never brought her to Jersey...

If he had allowed her to marry James...

None of this would have happened. She would never have been alone in the bay-side cottage, never encountered that reprobate man.

His leaving her alone on the isle, with no family, was the final insult.

He had left her to face everything alone.

Lessons would begin again in the morn. She would have to muster the courage to make it through the day, pretending all was well.

## Chapter Eighteen

Thomasse trudged down the pathway leading to Madame de Beauvoir's cottage. Three months had passed since that irrevocable day. Although her body had mostly healed and her mind had improved, a few lingering concerns remained.

The path curved, revealing a cottage nestled amongst a copse of trees. Larger than typical for common folk, the two-story structure boasted a real chimney, and a freshly hoed garden area awaited spring planting. Thomasse knocked on the door. It was answered by a maidservant who took her cloak before fetching Madame.

Dressed in a blue cotehardie and white wimple, Madame greeted her. "Thomasse! What a pleasant surprise. What brings you here?"

"A matter of delicacy," she whispered.

Madame beckoned Thomasse to follow, and led her through the cottage. Each room they passed contained furniture of quality. Thomasse schooled her countenance and bit her tongue. It would be rude to inquire how such wealth had been accumulated by the healer and her husband, the seigneur's reeve.

When they reached a small room in the back, Madame gestured toward the bed and drew up a wooden chair. "Sit, my child. Let us discuss the matter plainly."

Thomasse sat on the meager bed and adjusted her skirt. "Mostly I am healed." She glanced nervously at the table across the room, littered with a mortar and pestle, and several bottles filled with potions, herbs, and other plant specimens. "My flow has not returned, and I often take ill in the morn."

Madame pursed her lips. "Lie back so I may examine you."

Thomasse stretched out and Madame lifted the skirt of her cotehardie and kirtle, pressing and prodding until Thomasse winced.

"Does that pain you?" Madame asked.

"Just uncomfortable."

Madame pulled Thomasse's skirt down, then selected a cup from the table and handed it to her. "Piss in the cup. Call me when you are done." Madame quit the room, closing the door behind her.

Thomasse had seldom taken ill as a child, and the few times a surgeon had been called, he had never made such a request. For a moment, she questioned Madame's competency as a healer, then reminded herself Penna had expressed confidence in her. Nor had she heard rumors of Madame being a witch.

With the cup half full, Thomasse called out, "Finished!"

Madame returned. Her brow furrowed as she studied the contents. "Did you drink all the elixir I provided?"

Thomasse looked away. "A few times, but it tasted vile."

Madame pulled the chair closer and grasped Thomasse's hand. "I thought as much." She hesitated for a moment. "You are with child."

Thomasse jerked her hand free. "That cannot be."

The healer sighed heavily. "I wish it were not so."

"But I have no husband."

"But you have known a man."

Thomasse sprang from the bed. "You are wrong." As she fled the room, she heard Madame say, "I will come by the manor to check on you."

Her vision blurred, her mind numb, she stumbled out of the cottage and retraced her steps down the pathway, running with no destination in mind. She arrived at the water's edge, winded, her side aching.

She slowed to a walk as the initial shock of Madame's pronouncement sank in. Was she right? She had heard the whispers that a woman could only conceive when she took pleasure in the act. There had been no pleasure, only pain. But a healer would not lie about something of such import. Denial faded as logic crept in. All the signs, her missing flow, the sickness in the morning, pointed to the truth of it. Soon there would be no hiding it, and the gossip would be ruthless, her reputation in tatters, amid the endless speculation on who might be the father.

Thomasse wandered along the shore of St. Ouen's Bay, stopping now and again to gaze across the water, thinking of her home in Sussex. Stooping, she grabbed a handful of sand and let it slowly sift through her fingers. Had life gone differently, had they not been forced to flee, she would be married to Jack and the prospect of a child would be welcome news. To think once she had despised the thought of a marriage to him. Anything would be better than this.

In bygone days, she had heard murmurings of young ladies whisked away to a country estate, under the pretense of a much-needed reprieve from the demands of court. But here on Jersey, there was no place to hide until the babe arrived. Deemed an immoral woman, she would certainly be dismissed as Philippe's governess. And with no means of supporting a child, what was she to do? When her father returned, given his ambition, would he turn his back on her?

She weighed her choices. If she kept the child, she would be rejected by society—condemned to begging along the roadside or turning to harlotry. Or she could leave the babe on the doorstep of the church and pray a loving family took it in. But what if the babe ended up in the wrong hands and was used as a servant? She may be in a desperate situation, but the babe was still her flesh and blood. The thought of someone treating her child cruelly weighed heavily on her heart.

Marriage would solve her problems, but who would marry a woman thus dishonored? Or agree to raise a bastard child as his own? Her pride would never allow her to declare the father. Besides, chained in the dungeon, he could not provide for them.

Unbidden, scenes from that day flashed before her eyes, reigniting the old feelings—the fear, the helplessness, the mental anguish. After all these months, the physical pain had not diminished—as if a hundred daggers pierced her heart.

She continued walking; the waves breaking as the tide rolled in. She spotted the group of rocks where James had rescued her from drowning. A choked sob escaped her lips. If he had not saved her, she would have been spared all this pain and sorrow.

She wandered northward along the shore. The terrain steepened, and Grosnez Castle appeared up ahead. Irresistibly, she was drawn to the abandoned structure. Leaving the path, she picked her way through the brush and passed through the portcullis.

The wind whistled through the empty hallways as dry leaves tumbled across the floor, strewn with dried grass and splotched with bird droppings and dried mud. She ran her hands along the cold, rough stone walls as she climbed the stairs to the solar, drifting from room to room, all empty save one that held a broken cradle.

She quit the castle and continued up the steep path along the rocky northern coast. If only Agnes was here to comfort her, to wrap her arms around her like when she was a girl and assure her everything would be all right. Here, she was surrounded by people who scarcely knew her. She had no one to confide in, much less someone who would show her love and compassion.

Once she had known that with James—but she had lost that too. She stood near the edge of the cliff and stared into the dark water swirling below.

Huge waves smashed against the rocks. The burn of cold water would be less painful than this torment. The depths beckoned, promising an end to her misery, the answer to all her problems.

James slowed the roan to a trot as he neared the stable. Someone called his name, and he wheeled the horse around to find Madame de Beauvoir running toward him, clutching a cloak. He drew back the reins, bringing the roan to a halt. "What is it?"

Her breaths came quick and heavy. "Thomasse—came by the cottage—left distraught—forgot her cloak—not at the manor—never returned."

"Did she give any hint where she might have gone?"

Madame shook her head and handed James the cloak. "I fear for her safety."

"Why? What happened?"

"I cannot say, but someone must go find her."

James draped the cloak over the saddle. "I shall go."

"Thank you," Madame stepped back, gripping her side. "I knew I could depend on you."

A lump formed in his gut when he did not find her at the shore. Not only was it cold, but a maiden wandering alone—Thomasse knew the danger. He retraced the path leading to the manor. As he passed the chapel, he spotted Philippe's friend, William, sitting on the hillock watching the ships sail by. He nudged the roan forward. "William! Have you seen Thomasse?"

He pointed northward. "I saw her walk that way."

"How long ago?"

"'Tis been quite some time, but she has not returned."

James touched his coif. "Much obliged."

William scrambled up. "Do you want me to come with you?"

Not wishing to cause alarm, James held up the cloak. "That is unnecessary. I only seek to get this back to its rightful owner."

Heading back to the shore, James turned northward. Several fishing boats rested on the sand. Gulls circled overhead and shrieked as the fishers sorted their catch into baskets. He inquired of several if they had seen a young maiden pass by. When none had, his unease deepened.

The sandy shore turned rocky, and he steered the roan up the path that wended along the coastal cliffs. The wind picked up, and the temperature dropped. *What was Thomasse thinking, walking out in this chilly weather without her cloak? She could catch her death of cold.*

With each passing minute, the vise of fear tightened its grip. Grosnez Castle emerged ahead, and he hoped she had sought shelter there. He called her name, but received no answer. He rode to the entrance, and called her name again. Silence, except for the howling of the wind. Near the portcullis, he noted fresh footprints on the damp earth entering and leaving the abandoned castle.

He continued up the trail. Beyond, a blonde woman, skirt flapping in the wind, stood on the cliff. "Thomasse!" he shouted, as he urged the roan to a canter, then drew back the reins as he neared.

She turned, a haunted look in her eyes, then returned to staring down the cliff at the water churning about the rocks below.

"Thomasse, please do not do this."

He dropped the reins and vaulted from the saddle, racing to her side. "I brought your cloak."

"Let me be," she said, her voice cracking.

James draped the cloak over her shoulders. "Let me take you home."

"I have no home," she replied, her voice flat. "Go away. I wish to be alone."

"I will not leave you here."

What he would not give in this moment to protect this woman forever, to confess his undying love, but it would not be right. "You are not alone. There are those who care for you."

Thomasse stepped closer to the edge of the rocky cliff, her gaze fixed on the dark, swirling water below.

James reached out his hand, willing her to take it. "What of Philippe? He would be devastated at the loss of his governess and friend."

The rocks shifted and her foot slipped. James lunged, his heart pounding, and drew her away from the crag. A sob escaped her lips, and James wrapped his arms around her trembling body. He stroked her hair, waiting for her to calm.

"What happened?"

She shook her head against his shoulder, and he accepted that she was not ready to talk.

James pressed a light kiss on her hair. "Whatever has brought you to this point, I promise things will get better."

She drew away and wiped her eyes. "I do not see how."

"Come with me." He extended his hand. "Please."

She took it and allowed him to lead her to the horse.

Once astride the roan, he drew her up into the saddle and wrapped a protective arm about her waist. Taking up the reins, they rode slowly down the path toward the manor.

She relaxed against him. He tightened his hold on her, breathing in her scent of jasmine, hoping she felt his love. Maybe one day she would bare her soul, but for now, it was enough to know she was safe.

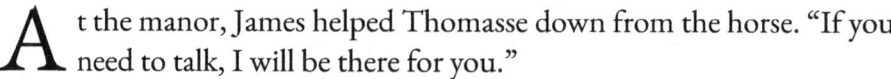

At the manor, James helped Thomasse down from the horse. "If you need to talk, I will be there for you."

She nodded and darted into the house. As she crossed the great hall, a servant pressed a letter into her hand. "This arrived a few hours ago."

Thomasse thanked the servant and raced up the stairs to her chamber, barring the door behind her. She set the letter on the table beside the bed and removed her cloak. She huddled near the fire, trying to chase the chill from her bones, terrified by where her thoughts had taken her.

Why did it have to be James who found her? Of all people, she did not want him to know how low she had sunk, the depths of her shame. If he knew the truth, that she carried the pirate's child, he would shun her, and she could not bear it.

The warmth thawed her distress, and she remembered the letter. Curious who could have sent it, she broke the seal, surprised to discover it was from her father.

> *Thomasse,*
>
> *I have arrived in France and am residing with our queen. I am happy to report Lord Jack is here among the exiles. He offers news of Eleanor and Arthur. They have settled near Oxford, although Arthur has turned traitor, joining forces with Edward, Duke of York.*
>
> *Good tidings. Lord Jack has been bestowed with the title of Earl of Devon. When this business is concluded, he means to claim your hand. Take courage. The wait will soon be over. King Henry will be restored, and you, my daughter, shall be a countess.*
>
> *Your loving father*

Thomasse refolded the letter and tucked it beneath the bolster. She had never dared hope this could happen. In England, she would be safe with her father's, or Lord Jack's, men-at-arms to protect her. Maybe then she could forget.

Her father remained ignorant of her ruination. If she gave up the child, no one would suspect until after the vows had been spoken.

Even then, perhaps the earl would suspect nothing amiss. Her future children would grow up with the same privileges that she had known; a fine education, beautiful clothes, horses, and a noble lineage. Safe. They would never face the hardship she had endured these past two years.

Unbidden, she heard Madame's words. "You may be barren." What if this child was her only chance to be a mother?

James whistled as he rubbed down the seigneur's black destrier. A hint of jasmine wafted through the stable. He glanced up to see Thomasse. A fortnight had passed since he had found her on the cliff. She stood just inside the stable door, twirling a lock of hair around her finger.

"You said if I needed to talk," she said in a hushed voice. "Is your offer still good?"

"Always." He set aside the brush and gestured for her to sit on the bench.

She perched on the edge, arranging and rearranging the folds of her skirt. "Promise not to think ill of me?"

"I could never," said James, taking a seat on the bench, leaving a comfortable distance between them.

"And not to tell anyone?"

"I am no gossip." Her question pained him, for he thought she knew him better.

"I am with child," she blurted out.

James flinched as if punched in the gut—the revelation dropping like a stone into a pond. His thoughts rippled and swirled as the weight of her confession hit him. Though he had suspected what had happened in the cottage, her disclosure removed any doubt.

"You think me a harlot." She must have misinterpreted his silence.

He schooled his countenance. "Do not assume what I think."

"The pirate is the babe's father." Thomasse slumped against the wall as though the admission required all her strength.

James slid his hand down the bench, stopping halfway between them, hoping she would take his hand, recognize the gesture as a sign he still loved her. "His actions do not determine who you are."

"Thank you for that kindness, but I fear when the Seigneur and Demoiselle learn the truth, they will turn me out." She turned toward James. "What will I do?"

"You can conceal your condition a few months more. Perhaps by then a solution will present." *Take my hand.*

"I should not have burdened you with this." Thomasse replied. "I am not your responsibility."

"If there is anything I can do to help?" James rose and offered her his hand. "This chill is not good for you or the babe. Let me take you back to the house."

Neither James nor Thomasse spoke as they crossed the green. What does a person say under such circumstances? While he could understand her distress, he could never fully comprehend the depths of her despair.

At the door, James said, "If you need anything, even just to talk—"

Thomasse nodded and disappeared within.

James stared at the closed door for a few moments, then returned to the stable, his heart heavy with regret. He grieved as he recalled how he had acquiesced to her father's wishes when Thomasse was prepared to stand up for their love. If her father had not forbidden their marriage, she would have been with him on that fateful morning. Even now, he would happily wed her, but she had not taken his hand, had not met him halfway. Perhaps more than her father stood between them.

## Chapter Nineteen

B uilt high on the rocks, the imposing castle of Mont Orgueil glistened in the afternoon sun. James rubbed his hands and stamped his feet, trying to stave off the chill as he waited on the bailey. Although it was a bit disconcerting to stand beneath the murder holes, the high stone walls protected him from the brisk winds off the water.

Nothing about this journey had gone as planned. Yesterday, he had accompanied the de Carteret family across the isle to attend an Easter celebration at Rozel Manor. During dinner, the captain of the French garrison and his henchman arrived unexpectedly, then demanded all the guests join them today for dinner.

Hence the original plan to return to St. Ouen this morning had been delayed until this afternoon. Now, the sun hung low in the western sky with no hint that the dinner would soon be over, meaning they would not reach home until after dark.

He sighed, and returned to the bench he had occupied earlier. Opening his pouch, he withdrew a block of wood and resumed whittling a whipping top for his younger siblings. But it was hard to concentrate, knowing the pirate was chained in the dungeon just a stone's throw away. As long as the man remained locked away, Thomasse was safe. And if justice were done, he would never draw another breath of fresh air.

James had just finished carving the groove for the leather cord when a soldier appeared, signaling for him to saddle the horses.

Slipping the toy and knife back into his pouch, he hurried to the stable and retrieved the horses. The mood of the family was pensive as they departed through the castle gate and turned onto the road leading west. James rode at the back of the party with Philippe, who was unusually quiet.

The sun sank behind the hills, and streaks of purple and orange peeked through the darkened clouds. "Beautiful sunset," James said.

Philippe blinked, as if pulled from deep thought. "I did not notice." Silence stretched between them again until Philippe blurted out, "James, they let the pirate go."

A chill wrapped around his heart as he struggled to make sense of Philippe's words. Surely he was mistaken. "How can that be?"

Philippe shrugged, looking a bit bewildered. "The Lady of Rozel pleaded for his release."

He fell silent again.

James pondered the news. Nothing made sense. What reason could the lady have to plead for mercy on behalf of such a vile man? And what of Thomasse? Although, she had made clear she was not his responsibility, this new information changed everything. Her personal safety could be at risk. He faced a dilemma. Should he warn her and risk her living in fear? Or hold his tongue? After all, there was no logical reason for the man to sojourn across the isle.

"How do I tell Thomasse?" Philippe asked.

"Do we need to?" James asked. "He would be a fool to return to St. Ouen."

"Perchance you are right," Philippe replied.

## Chapter Twenty

Thomasse hummed as she padded barefoot down the stairs to fetch breakfast. The stone floor was cold on her feet, but these days her ankles swelled and shoes were uncomfortable. Over the past month, her body had changed, the small mound had grown, thickening her waist. And she had felt the quickening—a flutter, like butterfly wings inside, and then the poke of a tiny finger.

Her stomach rumbled as she carefully navigated a path through the unwashed bodies of sleeping men, women, and children, grateful the stage where the stench made her retch had passed. At the sideboard, she selected a trencher and piled it with large portions of bread and cold pork.

Something tickled her neck, and she raised a hand to swat it away, stopping midair when strong arms encircled her waist.

"I have missed you, Thomasse."

The voice was soft against her ear. Her body trembled, and the trencher slipped from her hand. She would recognize that voice anywhere. John Hareford.

She pushed against his arms. "Get your hands off me!"

His tongue clicked. "Is that any way to greet your lover?"

She wanted to scream, fight, run, but she froze as his hands roamed her body, stilling over her belly. "You are with child."

She struggled and, breaking free, whirled to face him. He smirked, and she took strength from the sight of the angry scar on his left cheek. She slipped her hand into her pocket, and it closed around a kerchief. How she wished a spindle was hidden there. It would give her great pleasure to ram it into his cheek again and wipe that smug smile off his face.

"Why are you not in the dungeon?"

She sensed movement behind her.

Within moments, James stood beside her, his nostrils flaring. "Keep your filthy hands off my lady."

Hareford gripped Thomasse's arm with one hand and fondled the pommel of his sword with the other. "Your lady?" He sneered, his eyes filled with disdain as his gaze swept over James. "Is that a groom's duty—to raise what he cannot sire?"

The room buzzed with whispers. The confrontation had awakened many. Wrenching free from Hareford's grasp, she pleaded, "Keep your voices down."

She glanced toward the stairs leading to her chamber, and her eyes locked with the seigneur. Her face burned, and she wished she could sink through the floor.

Hareford cleared his throat and spat, the spittle hitting James and dripping down his cheek. "I despise a cuckold."

James's eyes narrowed, and his fists clenched.

Thomasse stepped between the two men. "Please, James! He is not worth it."

The seigneur approached. "What is going on here?"

Hareford bowed and stretched out his hand. "Seigneur de Carteret, we meet again. It has been too long."

De Carteret ignored the proffered hand. "What are you doing here? Your presence is unwelcome."

"Your friends informed me otherwise," Hareford replied.

Not waiting to be dismissed, James guided Thomasse from the room. "Damned isle custom—open doors that allow any reprobate to walk right in," he muttered.

At the bottom of the stairs, she mumbled. "Thank you for defending me."

She stumbled up to her chamber and flung herself onto the bed, drawing her legs close to her chest, her body shaking.

*Why did he come?* It was clear he felt no remorse for his actions. *While my life is in shambles, he walks free, going on with life as before.*

His return and declaration had forced her shameful secret into the open. She covered her face with her hands. She was not ready, even though nature would announce it soon enough. A cry escaped her lips at the thought of being the subject of cruel gossip. The shunning would begin.

She folded her arms around her belly, surprised by the mothering instinct the pirate's appearance had evoked. "I will protect you, little one," she whispered.

The door creaked open, and someone placed something on the table beside the bed. She caught the scent of citrus and cloves. Demoiselle Penna. "I brought you food."

Maybe she was not in physical danger, but she braced herself for the condemnation and the inevitable outcome. She would be dismissed.

"Look at me, Thomasse." Penna's voice was soft, almost comforting.

Thomasse shook her head.

"I am not leaving until we talk," Penna said.

"I shall pack my things and go," Thomasse whispered.

"You will do no such thing."

Thomasse met Penna's gaze. "What will become of me now I am ruined?"

"Put such thoughts from your head."

"But as a fallen woman, his lordship will deem me unworthy to teach your son—" A sob escaped her throat. "I am not fit for anything else."

"What happened was not your fault. I will speak with Seigneur de Carteret on your behalf." Penna pinched her lips. "He insists on an English tutor for Philippe, and with French soldiers occupying the isle, it will be impossible for him to engage another."

"Thank you for your kindness."

Penna perched on the edge of the bed. "Many women on this isle have suffered your same fate."

Thomasse's eyes widened. "Forsooth?"

"Between French soldiers, pirates, and loathsome swine which live amongst us, a woman must consider herself lucky to escape unscathed." Penna smoothed the bedding. "I have heard it helps to talk about it."

"How?" Thomasse asked. Her face burned as memories of that fateful morning returned. Things she would never tell a soul. Things she would rather forget. Things that still haunted her day and night. "It is too shameful to speak of aloud."

"Whenever you are ready."

Thomasse shuddered, knowing she could never confide in Penna. "I only wish I could quell the fear and the anger that rages within me."

"All in God's time. I shall pray for you." Penna rose and crossed to the door. "It has been a difficult morning. You are excused from teaching today."

Despite Penna's generous words, Thomasse remained torn. She loved being Philippe's governess, but did she truly want to stay? Could she ever feel safe here again? If only she could sail back to England and take refuge among her friends. But even as she considered the idea, she knew it was folly. Whether she arrived on their doorstep heavy with child, or with a babe in her arms and no husband to claim them, they would turn her away.

Such an escape would have to wait until after the child was born. But the idea of abandoning her child to be raised by another had begun to weigh on her conscience.

James stalked from the manor, trying to quell his fury. *How dare Hareford show his face in St. Ouen.* Certainly, James had not expected it. What could Hareford possibly gain by returning to the scene of his crime? James chided himself. His intentions had been honorable, but had he made a mistake by not warning Thomasse about the pirate's release? It would be a long while before he forgot her look of terror as Hareford groped her body.

He slid open the stable door, and Magnar nickered. He approached the magnificent black destrier and stroked his nose. "What do you say, Magnar? Did I do the right thing?" The stallion snorted and nuzzled his arm in response.

The clomp of boots sounded outside the stable. The conversation between de Carteret and Hareford must have been brief, and the seigneur must have skipped breakfast to arrive so quickly.

"Shall I ready Magnar, Seigneur?"

"Please. I shall ride to St. Ouen's Pond."

James fetched the saddle and bridle. When he returned, de Carteret said, "That was noble of you, coming to Thomasse's defense. Is it true she is with child?"

"Yes, Seigneur." James pulled the bridle over the horse's head.

De Carteret leaned against the wall, arms crossed, deep in thought. "She must wed."

James's stomach knotted. "You would not insist she marry that evil man?"

"Certainly not, but time is not on her side, and—given your declaration this morning—I thought, perchance—"

James lifted the saddle onto Magnar's back and tightened the strap. De Carteret's words left him unsettled. So much had happened since he and Thomasse's relationship had been torn asunder.

Thomasse's confession of her secret weeks earlier had stirred painful memories. Memories of Becca—her radiant smile, the joy they shared upon learning she was with child, followed by the unspeakable pain when he laid them to rest, their babe forever cradled in her arms. If Thomasse suffered the same fate—could his heart endure another loss?

The seigneur came to stand beside James as he loaded the saddlebag with fishing supplies. "You understand my meaning?"

"Yes, Seigneur," James said, as he strapped the saddlebag in place.

De Carteret mounted the stallion. "And—"

"I will consider it."

Once the seigneur was gone, James wrestled with his decision. The thought of Thomasse being turned out with nowhere to go was too much. Marriage would make her an honest woman and allow her to continue as Philippe's governess. And he had promised to help her.

Although his love for Thomasse had ne'er diminished, what of her? Since her father's departure, she had made no attempt to renew their relationship. Deep inside, he hoped his fears were unfounded, that she would welcome a renewal of their betrothal. Maybe they could find happiness, build a life together. But the choice had to be hers.

When the seigneur returned from fishing, James was ready with his answer. "I will, if she will have me."

117

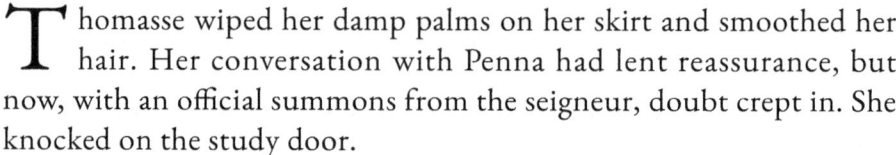

Thomasse wiped her damp palms on her skirt and smoothed her hair. Her conversation with Penna had lent reassurance, but now, with an official summons from the seigneur, doubt crept in. She knocked on the study door.

"Enter," de Carteret called out.

He stood before the hearth, tending the fire, and gestured for her to sit. She perched on the edge of the high-backed wooden chair, the same one she had sat on when he first offered her the position as Philippe's governess. More nervous now than that day, she tucked her hands beneath her to keep from fidgeting. With her father gone, no husband, and a babe on the way, her future rested on his decision.

De Carteret settled into his chair and placed his arms on the desk. "I have no complaint about Philippe's progress. However, given your situation, it would be unseemly to allow you to continue tutoring my son."

Thomasse gripped the edge of the chair. "I understand."

"I am prepared to retain your services under one condition."

She leaned forward. "Which is?"

"You must wed." He paused, giving her a moment to let his words sink in. "James has agreed to take you as his wife."

Her heartbeat quickened at the prospect, but just as quickly, doubts crept in, and the cold hand of dread wrapped around her chest. James had loved her once, but had he agreed to marry her out of pity—or at the seigneur's insistence? She did not want him to take her out of duty. But she did not wish to offend the seigneur.

"It is kind of James to make the sacrifice, but my father has promised me to another."

"Forsooth?" De Carteret's brows raised. "Might I inquire of whom you speak?"

She straightened. "The Earl of Devon."

The seigneur furrowed his brow. "He died two years past, leaving no heir."

"His younger brother, Lord Jack, is destined to replace him."

"If indeed you are betrothed, why has he not come for you?"

"It is complicated." She shifted in the chair. "My father happened upon him in France, and he reaffirmed his intentions."

"Ah!" De Carteret steepled his fingers and placed them on his chin. "Your father and the future earl are both in exile with Margaret d'Anjou."

Her head jerked backward. "You know?"

"It is my business to know these things."

Given the seigneur already knew her secret, she saw no reason to be anything but honest. "The wedding shall take place once King Henry returns to the throne."

"I admire your confidence." De Carteret rose and wandered over to the window and peered out for several minutes. "There is no way to put this delicately, but would Lord Jack honor the understanding if he discovered you bore a bastard child?"

Thomasse folded her arms over her belly, and a lump formed in her throat. "He need never know. I can place the child with a family to raise." Even as she spoke the words, she felt uneasy. Secrets had a way of being exposed, and the consequences of such a deception could be dire.

"Children are a blessing. Should King Henry's efforts prove unsuccessful, or your intended dies in battle, you will have relinquished your child for naught."

"I see no other possibility."

"I offered you a solution."

"Yes, but—"

De Carteret faced her, his gaze steady. "You are free to decline, but if you do, I will have no choice but to dismiss you."

She could only surmise her father's fury should he return and discover her wed to James, the one man he forbade her to marry. But the seigneur was right. Her choices were limited. And his remark that she could keep the child was a thought she had scarcely dared entertain.

De Carteret came and stood beside her, placing a hand on her shoulder. "It is unfortunate that society demands the appearance of virtue, when often that is all it is. I pray you understand. I seek what is best for you."

"Must I give an answer forthwith? Or may I have time to consider?"

"Take a day or two. Just remember, time is not your friend. James is a good man. He will treat you kindly."

Thomasse rose and made her way to the door.

"Before I go, might I inquire how the pirate escaped the dungeon? Why did he come to St. Ouen?"

"The Lady of Rozel pleaded for his release, and the captain granted her petition. Since his parole, Hareford has styled himself a rebel leader, intent on ousting the French. I fear two of my fellow seigneurs have been swayed and sent him to persuade me of the soundness of his cause. But I see him for the fraud that he is," de Carteret said. "It is most unfortunate that he arrived under cover of night. My men-at-arms did not know him. Should he come again, I have ordered them to arrest him."

"Gramercy, seigneur."

Thomasse softly shut the door behind her and trudged up the stairs to her chamber, each step weighted by the burden of the choices she must make.

Thomasse traced the intricate carving on the back of her brush—the first gift from James when she arrived on the isle. It all seemed so long ago now, when she had imagined James brushing her hair, placing a kiss on her bare shoulder, and whispering words of love. But that dream had ended long ago. It was de Carteret who had asked James to marry her—he had not offered. It hurt to think of James wedding her out of obligation.

She pulled at the cord that bound her braid, freeing her tresses to flow down her back, and ran the brush down the length of her hair. She turned away from the mirror, unable to look at her reflection any longer. The seigneur was right. No honorable man would marry her now that her virtue was gone. The pirate had stolen more than her innocence.

She laid the brush back on the dressing table. The decision put before her could not be delayed.

Above all, she wanted to be safe, something she had known in her father's house, and something she could count on if she married Jack. But the seigneur had pointed out the uncertainty of that future.

Did she expect too much? Perhaps there was no assurance against harm in this world.

She shivered at the thought of the French soldiers who prowled the parish at night. If she declined de Carteret's solution, she would be turned out and become easy prey. If they used her as a hedge whore—she shuddered.

What had Agnes said so long ago? Something she had brushed off as foolish talk, about what a girl should want in a husband—"a man who listens, who is gentle and kind, he is the one worth cleaving to." Now she understood better the wisdom in those words.

Although he was a man of humble birth, she had always been able to confide in James. He never dismissed her thoughts or feelings; with him she had always felt safe. He was steady, and their marriage would give her a chance for a future.

Her hand caressed her belly—a chance to be a mother to her child.

Maybe—just maybe—he would come to love her again.

Yes. She would marry James.

## Chapter Twenty-One

James scanned the bay-side cottage, pleased by the transformation. Despite a fortnight of heavy rains, his mother had swept away the cobwebs and strewn fresh rushes and lavender across the dirt floor. A mat, large enough for two, replaced the ones Thomasse and her father had used.

On the table, he placed his wedding gift. Upon receiving word that Thomasse had agreed to marry, he had spent many hours carving intricate designs into the chest. He traced the heart-shaped lock with his finger. A twinge of guilt pricked his conscience; guilt at moving on, guilt that he might forget his first love.

"I am sorry, Becca," he whispered. "But 'tis time I bid farewell to the life we will never have." His throat tightened. "Thomasse is a good woman. I just hope I am worthy of her."

A warmth enveloped his body, and the fragrance of gorse filled the air—the yellow flowers Becca loved. He closed his eyes, inhaling the scent, and heard her whisper, "You are worthy."

He wrapped his arms around himself as if he could embrace her one last time. "I will always love you."

Taking one last look around, he quit the cottage, shutting the door on his past. When he next opened it, a whole new life would await.

Thomasse stared out the window of her chamber. Rain pounded against the windows, and fog made it impossible to see even the green below. In the fortnight since she agreed to wed James, the rain had been unrelenting. It was difficult not to think the storm forebode a troubled future.

Moving to the dressing table, she brushed and braided her hair before the looking glass. The eyes of a poor working girl stared back at her. All resemblance to the girl who attended that last party in England had vanished. She had been so flighty then, gossiping with friends, and believing herself so in love with a man she had hardly thought of since. She could not imagine ever being so frivolous again.

A knock sounded on the door. "James has arrived," said a maidservant.

"Tell him I shall be right down," Thomasse called back.

She crossed to the wardrobe and pulled out the blue cotehardie and donned it quickly. There was no special gown for her wedding day, but at least it was not gray.

She took one last look in the mirror. Within the hour, she would be a married woman—her descent from the status of her birth to a permanent servant class complete. She donned her cloak and quit the room.

James waited at the bottom of the stairs. When their eyes met, her breath caught, realizing the implications of this next step. As his wife, he had the right to claim her—the way the pirate had. Bile rose in her throat, and she fought the urge to flee back to her chamber.

James smiled, ascended the stairs, and offered her his arm. "You look lovely."

She trembled, but she stiffened her spine. This was necessary to keep her position as governess.

She hooked her hand through his arm. As they crossed the great hall, the servants and men-at-arms shouted ribald comments. What seemed like harmless fun at other weddings only magnified her fears.

On the half-hour walk to St. Ouen's Parish Church, they dodged raindrops and skirted the large puddles formed by two weeks of relentless rain.

At the church, they stood on the porch and declared their vows—just her and James before God. She had insisted upon marrying here, for it felt sacrilegious to proclaim themselves married anywhere else.

"I take thee, Thomasse, to be my lawfully wedded wife." James's mouth ticked as he pushed the ring he had carved onto her finger.

Thomasse's thoughts tumbled. What did he find so funny about marrying her?

He brushed back a strand of her wet locks. "Look at us, dripping wet. Probably the most sodden bride and groom the parish has ever known."

Water pooled on the stone threshold beneath their feet. A droplet trickled down James's forehead and hung off the tip of his nose. Thomasse smiled, then laughed, truly laughed for the first time in months. Her heart soared, for she had oft wondered if she would ever laugh again.

James leaned in to kiss her. Her first instinct was to draw back, but they had just exchanged vows. He was entitled to seal their union with a kiss. His lips touched hers, soft and gentle.

Her stomach fluttered, just as it had in times past. All those feelings she had suppressed burst forth anew. She sighed contentedly as his arms encircled her waist and drew her close. Of their own accord, her hands travelled along his muscular chest, moving upward until her fingers intertwined in his hair, her whole body begging for the kiss to deepen.

"Let me take you home," James said, his voice husky.

Not sure where that was, she chose to trust.

Hand in hand, they strolled along the shoreline of St. Ouen's Bay, stopping to share passionate kisses and dance in the rain. They headed toward the hills and stopped at the doorway of the bay-side cottage. All her newfound happiness drained away. She stared at James, soaking wet, and suddenly it was not him standing there, but the pirate.

She yanked her hand away. "Why did you bring me here?"

"This is our home," James replied, his voice wavering.

"No!" Thomasse stumbled back as the world spun around her. "I—I will not go in there!"

James looked perplexed. "Where else should we go? The stable?"

"Take me to the manor house," she choked out.

"As you wish," James replied, his words clipped.

She ran along the path leading over the hillock to the manor house. She opened the door and slammed it in James's face without a word. Once in her chamber, she barred the door.

Fists clenched, she paced the room. How could he do this to her? He knew what had happened there. Behind the door of the bay-side cottage lay the memories she was desperate to bury. How long would that one ordeal cast its shadow over her future?

J ames stormed down the path to the stable. What had possessed him to think Thomasse would ever return his love? That she would make a good wife? 'Twas the way of the gentry to toy with the hearts of those deemed beneath them.

He had taken the risk, opened his heart, and she had played him for a fool—returning his kiss after their vows, laughing with him in the rain, making him believe her regard for him. But it was all a farce. When the time came to truly become man and wife, she had rejected him—cruelly and without hesitation.

Was she in her chamber now, laughing at him, despising the love he had so eagerly bestowed?

He saddled the roan and pressed the mare into a canter, heedless of the muddy roads. He rode toward St. Helier, for every other pathway was tainted with memories—her easy laugh, stolen kisses amongst the trees, holding her in her moment of deepest despair.

The wind whipped his cloak and his hands tightened on the reins as he nudged the roan into a gallop. All the hours he had spent carving the chest, imagining their future together, had just been folly on his part.

The seigneur and Thomasse should be satisfied. Their marriage secured her respectability. Only he was left to pay the price for foolishly risking his heart.

T he next morning, when Thomasse entered the schoolroom, she found Philippe seated on the window ledge, basking in the sunshine.

"Good morning," he smiled brightly. "The sun finally shines today."

Unbidden, her eyes welled. It was anything but a good morning, the turmoil of the previous day's emotions still unsettled.

Philippe slid off the ledge and stepped toward her. "Are you unwell?"

She turned away and dashed a hand across her cheek. It would not do for Philippe to see her cry. "Never better. Let us begin your lessons."

"You might as well tell me for the servants gossip," Philippe said. "It is better if I hear it from you."

She pulled a kerchief from her pocket and dabbed at her nose, then extended the hand bearing the wedding band James had placed there only yesterday.

His eyes widened. "What? When? Who?"

"James and I married yesterday at St. Ouen's Parish Church."

"Really? I did not know you were betrothed."

"Your father insisted." A tear slid down her cheek. "If I refused, he would dismiss me as your governess."

Philippe frowned. "Why would my father do that?"

"You may be too young to understand—what happened at Christmas—there was little chance I would ever marry." She sighed. "I should be grateful James agreed."

"You make marriage sound horrible. So, why marry at all?"

Thomasse placed a hand over her belly. "Because I am with child."

"Then I must congratulate you."

She shook her head. "Please do not. I must accept that life has trampled on my dreams. I have paid dearly for the sins of my father."

Philippe wrapped his arms around her. "What did he do that you should suffer so?"

Footsteps sounded in the hall and Penna glided into the room, dressed in an emerald riding habit and white wimple. "Thomasse, I require Philippe's company."

"Of course, Demoiselle." Thomasse curtsied, then busied herself with organizing the books on the table.

"Come, Philippe." Penna beckoned for him to follow, then paused at the door. "You are dismissed for the day."

Thomasse escaped to her chamber, grateful to be spared the need to answer Philippe's question. Besides, she needed time to think. In the light of the sunny morning, she regretted her treatment of James. How could he know the sight of the bay-side cottage would send her reeling?

No one seemed to understand. Even Penna, though compassionate at first, soon acted as though the incident should be behind her—unaware that a word or gesture could provoke memories, sending her back into the cottage, reliving the nightmare. Perhaps she possessed some flaw of character that made it impossible to let go and move forward.

That was not James's fault. He had always been kind—gentle—patient. Maybe, if she confided her deepest secrets, he would understand. But speaking them aloud would be humiliating.

She could never tell him how at night she sometimes woke from a nightmare to the feel of the pirate's rough hands in places no man had touched before.

Or the wicked smile on the pirate's face when he perceived he had stolen her virtue—the gift that should have belonged to James.

The guilt that it was her fault. She had invited him into the cottage. That somehow she had led the pirate to believe she desired it.

How when people looked at her she felt like the word harlot was tattooed on her forehead.

Of how she felt—tarnished, broken, and unlovable.

If he knew it all, knew her shame—could he ever stand to look at her again?

## Chapter Twenty-Two

A moon passed before Thomasse next saw James. She visited the stable nearly every day, but he was never to be found. She feared he was avoiding her, but the other servants assured her that his duties demanded his presence elsewhere.

Finally, on a warm June evening, she found him mucking out the stalls. "James, I—"

He paused and leaned on the pitchfork, waiting, not saying a word.

She swallowed; her prepared words vanished like fog in the morning sun. "The weather is much improved since we last spoke."

James said nothing, his eyes hooded. Her heart skipped. He looked incredibly handsome with his hair disheveled, sweat glistening on his brow. She had expected anger in those amber eyes, but there was only quiet forbearance.

"I owe you an apology. My behavior was unbecoming of a lady."

"What truly brings you here?"

"I have come to make amends," Thomasse replied. "I just do not understand why you took me to the cottage."

"It belongs to me. That is our home."

"How?" The words caught in her throat. "When my father and I arrived, you told me the old man who lived there had died."

"That is true. I inherited the cottage from my grandfather."

Her gaze darted about the stable. "But you sleep here?"

James sagged against the stall gate. "After Becca died, I could not bear to go back there. I hoped we could make new memories—" His voice cracked. "Replace the bad with something good."

She rested a hand on his arm. "I am sorry. It seems that place holds painful memories for both of us."

He ran his fingers through his hair. "Dear God, forgive me. I did not consider how going there would affect you."

"Of course, I forgive you." Thomasse stepped back. "I need you to understand—I am not ready to make it my home. I may never be."

His grip tightened on the pitchfork. "Why must you toy with me? One moment you ask forgiveness, the next you reject me." He returned to pitching soiled rushes from the stall, and the stable filled with the scent of freshly disturbed dung. The tension in his muscles and the force of his movements betrayed his frustration.

"That is not my intent. I hope we can be friends."

"That is not enough for me. I want a true wife or nothing. You have what you want, a ring on your finger, your future as governess secured." James leaned the pitchfork against the wall. "Excuse me."

Thomasse watched as he stalked from the stable and disappeared down the path. She walked slowly back to the manor house, fearing she had only made things worse. In all her youthful dreams, this was not how she pictured marriage.

Thomasse threw herself into preparing and teaching lessons for Philippe and William. On this warm summer day, Philippe and William refused to settle down.

"Can we pack a basket and go for an outing?" Philippe asked.

Thomasse wiped the sweat from the back of her neck. "You can play once your lessons are complete."

"It has been a long while since we had an outdoor lesson. And William never." She noted the mischievous look in Philippe's eyes, realizing there would be no deterring him. "We can study plants and catch lizards."

The babe squirmed, and her heart squeezed. Perhaps it was trying to tell her the room was too muggy, that the cool breeze off the bay was the ideal way to spend the afternoon. Her hand drifted to her belly, amazed at how much she had come to love someone she had yet to meet.

"That sounds like a wonderful plan. I will ask the cook to prepare a basket while the two of you put away your things. Bring the nets, and I will meet you on the hillock."

"Yes!" William jumped out of his chair. "You are the best governess."

She laughed. "I will remind you of that next time you complain about your reading assignment."

Quitting the room, she lumbered down the stairs. At least, that was how she felt nowadays. With her expanding girth, she was no longer light on her feet, and she tired more quickly.

At the cookhouse, she was not surprised when the cook handed her an already prepared basket of victuals. *Philippe.* She should have guessed by the look in his eyes earlier that he had pre-planned it.

When she reached the crest of the hillock, the boys were practicing fighting, their wooden swords clacking as they feinted, blocked, and parried. She found an even spot beneath an alder tree, not far from where the boys had left their nets.

Opening the basket, she laid out the blanket along with a repast of cold chicken, cheese, berries, bread, a flask of ale, and another of milk. The amount of food seemed excessive for three people, but maybe the cook figured two growing boys and a woman quick with child required larger portions. When she withdrew four trenchers and four tankards, Philippe's purpose became clear.

The grass swished, and Thomasse's gaze darted toward the noise. James stood nearby, his face blank—he looked tired.

She smiled nervously. "Hello, James. This is a pleasant surprise." She patted the blanket. "Come, join us. There is plenty."

"I must decline," he replied. "Philippe asked me to meet him here, that is all."

Philippe called out. "William, James and Thomasse are here." The two boys stopped fighting and raced over, tossing their swords down beside the nets.

She gave Philippe a stern look. "Did you arrange this?"

His body wiggled with excitement. "I did. You and James are my two favorite people—" Philippe looked at his best friend, "after William. I do not know what happened, but I want you to be friends again."

James glared at Philippe. "It was wrong of you to interfere." He turned to Thomasse. "If you wish to speak with me, come to me yourself." He turned on his heel and began striding down the hillock.

"James," Thomasse called after him. "Please, stay. Truly, I was not a party to this. Let us not disappoint the boys after they went to so much effort."

James returned and settled beneath the tree. The boys chattered on about who was better at swordplay, then about their plans to hunt lizards and bugs after they ate.

Thomasse filled the trenchers and handed them around. She watched James through lowered lashes as they ate, trying to assess his mood. As the meal progressed, he relaxed, teasing the boys, and offering suggestions on the best way to capture voles and dragonflies.

When the boys finished eating, they grabbed their nets and raced down the hillock toward the stream that wended behind the stable and the chapel.

James drained his tankard of ale and stood. "Thank you for the victuals."

Thomasse reached out to him. "Do not go. We have many things to discuss."

"Like—"

She took a deep breath. After how badly she had blundered last time, she had no idea how the conversation would go. "The babe will arrive in a few months. Whether a boy or a girl, it will need a father."

James heaved a sigh and sat back down. With Thomasse, he never knew what to expect. She had changed since she first arrived in Jersey, even from when they had first declared their love. When they became betrothed two springs ago, she was the one who suggested they lie together, declare themselves man and wife, and face the consequences together. He was the one who insisted on following the rules—getting her father's blessing and the seigneur's permission. But now they were married, she had made it clear she had no intention of living with him as his wife.

And now she was requesting he be a father to her child. "How do we build a life together, become a family, when you refuse to live as my wife?"

"I have agonized many a night over our situation." Her mouth pinched. "It is not you I have rejected, but living in that cottage."

"So what do you propose?" James asked. "There is not room to live with my parents, and I doubt you would be amenable to sleeping in the stable. With my status as a groom, the seigneur and demoiselle would never agree to my entering their private family quarters."

"I am fully aware of the rules of propriety," Thomasse replied. "That places us at a difficult crossroads. Are there no other options?"

James's jaw tightened. "Most people have not the luxury of abandoning their homes because of painful memories. What do you suggest?"

Thomasse shrugged. "I do not know." She picked at her skirt, brushing away the crumbs. She needed to be bold, to be honest with him.

"I wish you could understand how overwhelmed I feel—the pressure of teaching two boys, becoming your wife, and soon, a mother." Her voice lowered. "And I am still trying to make peace with what happened that day."

He reached for her hand, his heart melting. "I could understand if you would just help me."

A tear glistened in her eye, and she ducked her head. "I fear if I speak plainly, you will despise me. You deserve better than me."

James placed a finger under her chin and lifted her face until she met his gaze. "Whole or broken—I love you. We can work this through together."

## Chapter Twenty-Three

The warm August sunshine filtered through the trees, dappling the dusty roadway. On either side, ripe rye swayed in the breeze, heavy heads ready for harvest. Thomasse had hesitated when James invited her to the St. Lawrence Faire, but now she was happy she had accepted.

Over the past several weeks, they had gradually worked through their misunderstandings, returning to a companionable relationship. Conversation flowed easily between them, reminiscent of earlier days when they first pledged themselves to one another.

Hot, her feet tired, Thomasse said, "Let us rest a while."

They sat on the low stone wall beside the roadway. She took a long draught from James's leather costrel, the water cooling her parched tongue. She handed it back, wiping her mouth on her sleeve.

The love in his eyes made her heart flutter, and she slipped her hand into his. The babe kicked, and she placed his hand on her belly which now protruded like a ball. "Did you feel it?"

The babe kicked again, and James grinned. "I long for the day when we welcome our child into the world."

Her heart swelled at his words, that he would acknowledge this child as his own. "What do you wish for? A boy or a girl?"

He kissed her cheek. "Either will be a blessing, although a girl with blond curls like her mother would surely steal my heart."

Thomasse smiled. "You mean to flatter me, and I will not protest. I have decided if it is a girl, I shall name her Joanna, after my mother. If it is a boy, I will name him Robert, after my brother."

"Lovely names," James said. "I would like to ask Philippe to be the godfather."

"What a wonderful idea!"

James stood and proffered his hand. "Let us continue on lest we miss the faire."

As they approached, the crowd grew denser and faint strains of a hurdy-gurdy floated on the breeze. Brightly colored booths lined the field and the aroma of roasted mutton and goose filled the air. Thomasse's stomach rumbled, and the babe squirmed, probably as eager to sample the food offerings as its mother.

Vendors hawked their merchandise: fabrics, pottery, candles, and exotic spices. How pleasant to handle the soft silks, velvets, and furs again, to rub lotion into her hands, and look at the latest fashion in shoes. But, aside from replenishing her jasmine oil, she would only look.

Handling such luxuries, her thoughts flitted briefly to the friends she had left behind. She wondered if Eleanor and Arthur were happy, and what had become of Maud now that King Henry and Queen Margaret were in exile.

She looped her hand through James's arm and pressed in close to his side, so the jostling mob could not separate them. They feasted on roasted goose legs and sipped spicy mulled wine while they watched men play at bowls. Moving on, they cheered the men and boys competing in archery.

But what delighted Thomasse most was the puppet shows and the troubadours singing tales of chivalry and love. Wandering hand in hand, she sensed the bond deepening between them. Most gratifying was the pride he took in introducing her as his wife.

The sun hung low in the western sky, signaling the need to depart if they wished to reach St. Ouen before darkness fell. The path passed the animal yard. Pigs snuffled in their pens, and cows lowed in the barn. A group of men, engaged in boisterous conversation, stumbled out and gathered near the trough.

A voice rang out above the din of the crowd. "Hoy, James. Still chasing after that harlot?"

Thomasse froze mid-step. Hareford. That voice would haunt her forever.

The crowd hushed; all eyes on them.

James's grip on her hand tightened. "Do not speak of my wife thus."

Hareford lurched toward them, the stench of ale heavy on his breath. "Your wife!" His lip curled. "I will see hell before I let some country churl raise my child."

Her stomach knotted, and her face burned. She shrank back, clutching her belly—a futile attempt to hide what all could plainly see.

James grabbed Hareford's tunic. "You filthy knave—"

Hareford guffawed. "Fool! Mark my words, I will take what is mine."

James shoved Hareford. "Stay away from her!"

Hareford jabbed a finger in James's face. James bit down hard. Hareford yelped and tumbled backward into the trough. "Fie! He bit my finger." He flailed and sputtered, sloshing water onto the ground. "Get me out of here or there will be hell to pay."

Laughter erupted from the crowd.

James raised his fist. "You are right where you belong—with the swine!"

Determined to escape the gawking crowd, Thomasse lifted her skirt and ran. Due to the awkwardness of her large belly, her progress was slow and clumsy. The blood pounded in her head. Never would she allow that man to touch her precious child.

Rapid footfalls sounded behind her. "Thomasse, wait!" James called.

She whirled about, her body trembling. "Why is that man here?"

"How should I know?" James reached for her.

"Do not touch me!" Thomasse said. "I have never been so humiliated. I wish we had never come!"

James's face fell. "I am sorry. Had I known—"

Her breaths came fast and heavy. "He is going to take my child."

He caught her arm and turned her to face him. "I promise that will not happen. You are protected, not only by me, but also by the seigneur."

His attempt at reassurance did not quell her distress. They walked in silence for over an hour, the air crackling with tension. Sweat trickled down her neck; her tired back and feet ached, but she refused to ask to rest.

As they neared St. Ouen's Parish, a sharp pang curved across her belly. She pursed her lips and exhaled sharply, certain it was just one of those strange sensations that came when carrying a child. Several minutes passed when another, stronger pain gripped her. She moaned and doubled over, waiting for it to pass.

James wrapped her arm around his shoulder. "Something is wrong." He lifted her in his arms and carried her the remaining distance to the bay-side cottage.

"Not here," Thomasse gasped as another pain began.

"Would you prefer the stable?"

She shook her head.

James carried her inside, laid her gently on the mat, and covered her with a blanket. "I shall fetch water."

She grabbed his hand. "Do not leave me."

He kissed her lightly on the forehead. "I shall make haste."

When he returned, his costrel refilled, she took a long draught. Another pain crossed her back. "My hour has come," she panted. "Hurry! Fetch Madame de Beauvoir."

# Chapter Twenty-Four

James slumped against the alder tree and pulled off his coif. The cool bay breeze ruffled his hair—a refreshing respite after the stifling heat inside the cottage. He had spent all night at Thomasse's side, holding her hand as her contractions strengthened. He would have stayed despite the hurtful words she had hurled at him—screaming for him not to touch her, blaming him for her early travail, and demanding he leave and never return.

When Madame de Beauvoir finally arrived, he had been summarily ordered from the cottage.

Youthful voices invaded his brooding. Philippe and William crested the hillock, racing toward the cottage. When they reached the door, Philippe handed something to William then skipped over to join James. "How is Thomasse?" he asked.

A cry escaped the cottage, fading to a soft moan. James hunched his shoulders, fighting the urge to cover his ears. The sound was all too familiar.

Philippe leaned against the trunk beside James. "Tell me."

"The babe is early. This is my fault."

"How are you to blame?"

"I wanted her to attend the faire." James hesitated, suppressing the tears that threatened. "I wanted to show off my bride. Is that so wrong?"

Philippe frowned. "Not at all. She is very pretty."

"I should have foreseen the pirate would be there." James kicked his foot hard against the tree. He deserved the pain for his stupidity.

"Fie!" Philippe said through clenched teeth. "What happened?"

137

"He threatened to take her child. Nigh everyone at the faire heard. Thomasse was mortified. On the way home, her travail began." James twisted his coif. "If they both die, I have only myself to blame."

"I have heard the servants say babes come when they come," Philippe said, his demeanor serious.

Despite his worry, James smiled wryly at Philippe's grownup behavior.

The cottage door creaked open, and a hand shot out. William placed the object in it and scurried over to join them.

"Did you give your mother the statue?" Philippe asked.

William nodded. "James, do not worry. St. Margaret will protect Thomasse."

James pushed away from the tree and paced, wearing a path in the sand. "I should have refused when I had the chance."

"Refused what?"

"To marry her." A sob escaped him. "She has lost a lot of blood, and the babe is too early." His voice cracked. "Just like Becca..."

"You love her," Philippe said.

James nodded as tears began to flow. "But I fear she hates me."

"I do not believe it."

"She wants me gone." He winced as another cry pierced the air. "If by some miracle she survives, I will grant her wish."

Philippe put a hand on James's shoulder. "If you are not there, who will protect Thomasse and her babe?"

"They will be fine without me," James muttered.

"Maybe she is just scared," Philippe replied.

"Or angry!" William blurted out. "Sometimes I say things I do not mean when I am upset. I suspect she is sorry."

They waited, huddled in the tree's shade, making little conversation. As the tide rose, the crashing of the waves mingled with the shriek of the gulls and Thomasse's anguished cries. Time passed agonizingly slowly. James's mind drifting again and again to the day Becca and their babe had died. If God called Thomasse home too—it would break him forever.

William gasped. "I almost forgot. Mother said someone must tell the priest to be ready to baptize the babe, no matter the time, day or night."

"I cannot leave," James said. "Can one of you go?"

"I shall go." William dashed off, quickly disappearing over the hillock.

Several minutes later, Penna arrived, accompanied by two maidservants carrying baskets of clean linens.

Philippe hastened to greet his mother. "Can you get news of Thomasse and the babe?"

She glanced at James. "Poor man. I shall see what I can do." She disappeared into the cottage with the maidservants.

Shortly after, a maidservant emerged only to report what they already knew—the labor was long and difficult. As the sun sank below the water, the faint wail of a babe broke the stillness.

James blew out a breath and hugged Philippe. "The babe lives. Will you be the godfather?"

"Me? I am just a boy."

"So—"

"Yes! Yes!" Philippe shouted.

The door opened, and Madame de Beauvoir appeared. "It is a girl! Her name is Joanna."

James crossed himself. "Praise St. Margaret. How is Thomasse?"

"Very weak, and the babe is tiny. They need your prayers that the grave may not claim them."

James tried to push his way inside, but Madame blocked his path. "I want to see them."

"Thomasse is tired and needs her rest." Her tone was gentle, yet firm. "The babe must be christened forthwith."

"Is that necessary? I heard her cry; the lungs sound strong. Surely there is hope?"

"As long as they breathe, there is always hope. But in these matters, it is best to prepare for the worst."

James staggered backward as if struck. The earth swirled beneath him and everything faded. He felt himself falling, until a grip on his arm pulled him back to consciousness.

Philippe offered James a drink from his costrel, and James steadied.

Madame reappeared and placed the swaddled babe in his arms. "Go quickly."

James gazed into his daughter's face, her eyes shut tight and her tiny mouth screwed up. Whatever came to pass between him and Thomasse, he would always think of her that way.

He tucked her close to his chest and walked to the church, praying the strength of his love would be enough to keep her tiny heart beating.

# Chapter Twenty-Five

"How do Thomasse and Joanna fare?" Philippe asked as James hoisted him into the saddle.

"I trust they are recovering," James replied.

He slapped the gelding on the haunch. Philippe wobbled as the horse moved forward and out of the stable.

James grabbed a pitchfork from the back corner and occupied himself loading the mangers with hay—any task to keep his mind off what was happening at the cottage.

It had been five long days since Joanna entered the world, and the only word of their welfare had come from a maidservant three days previous. How strange—and painful—not to know how his wife and daughter fared. But after Thomasse demanded he leave and not return, he had not expected to be told aught of them. He took comfort that no one had come bearing bad tidings.

Rushes crackled. James recognized the maidservant who had attended Joanna's birth.

"Madame de Beauvoir requests you come to the cottage forthwith," she said.

His chest tightened. The news could not be good, or Madame would not have sent for him.

His feet felt heavy as bricks as he hurried along the path to the cottage. At the crest of the hillock, he paused. Everything looked peaceful. Too peaceful. He continued down the path and tapped on the door.

Madame opened it and waved him inside. "Many thanks for coming with such haste."

Thomasse slept peacefully on a mat beside the fire. The maidservant sat in a chair in the back corner holding the swaddled Joanna. Nothing appeared to be amiss.

"How do they fare?"

"Both are on the mend, but not yet out of danger." Madame gestured for James to sit with her at the table. "Demoiselle Penna requires her maidservant, and I must be about my other patients."

James's mind eased. "So Thomasse is strong enough to care for herself and the babe?"

"Unfortunately, no," she replied. "As husband and father, I fear the task of caring for them must fall on you."

"After her declaration, do you think it wise?"

Madame placed a hand over his. "Women in travail say many things they do not mean."

James shook his head, unconvinced but resigned. "What must I do?"

She pointed to the kettle hanging over the fire. "I have prepared a large pot of broth. Feed it to Thomasse until she is able for solid food. Joanna grows stronger, and must be fed as well. The maidservant will instruct you."

Rising, she collected her satchel and headed toward the door. "If either Thomasse or Joanna takes a turn for the worse, fetch me."

When Madame was gone, the maidservant carefully laid the babe in the cradle beside the chair. James approached, and the maidservant placed a finger to her lips. He leaned over the cradle, his heart melting at the sight of his sleeping daughter. Her pale lashes were barely visible against her milky skin and her little pink mouth made sucking noises as if she were still feeding.

The maidservant showed him how to dip the cloth into the milk and twist it to fit into the babe's mouth, not unlike how he had fed many a newborn foal.

"I am much obliged," James said when the maidservant departed.

The next several days passed quickly, with so many duties of which James was not accustomed—feeding Joanna, rocking her when she cried, and changing her soiled swaddling bands. Fortunately, she slept a lot, giving him time to gather wood, fetch water from the nearby stream, and wash the soiled bands.

When Thomasse awoke, he held her head while she sipped the broth Madame had prepared. In her weakened state, her words of gratitude gave him hope that Madame and William had been right—that she regretted her harsh words.

Under his care, mother and daughter gained strength. Within a sennight, Thomasse was able to sit in a chair and hold her child, and take on more responsibilities, allowing James to resume his duties in the stable. Returning home at night, it warmed his heart to watch Thomasse coo and kiss Joanna's fuzzy head. Contentment permeated the cottage, and hope sprang anew that they could make this place a home—become a real family.

It was a fortnight after Joanna's birth, when de Carteret appeared in the stable demanding all the horses be saddled up. A matter of utmost gravity required his presence across the isle. James was to accompany him and the family.

James hastened to the cottage. "I came by to let you know that I will be gone a few days."

"Where are you going?" Thomasse asked.

"To Rozel Manor," James replied. "The Seigneur of Rozel and his friend, the Reverend of St. Martin's Church, have been arrested and charged with conspiracy against the French garrison. The Lady of Rozel has requested Seigneur de Carteret's help."

James bent and kissed Thomasse's cheek and that of the babe. "I have asked a servant to check in on you."

With that, he quit the cottage, heart heavy. In her condition, it would not be easy for Thomasse to manage everything on her own.

# Chapter Twenty-Six

The following morning, a servant arrived, just as James had promised, carrying a bucket of milk.

"Is there any word about Seigneur de Carteret's friends?" Thomasse asked.

"Only that he failed to gain their release. Rumor has it the garrison is searching for a third conspirator, that man Hareford," she said, setting the bucket on the table. "He is a desperate man. Keep your door barred."

"Many thanks for the warning," Thomasse replied.

"Unless you need something else, I shall be on my way."

Thomasse rose. "Nothing else." She followed the maid to the door, and barred it behind her.

She grabbed Joanna and tucked her in close. Her body trembled as she recalled the pirate's words at the faire. "I will see hell before I let some country churl raise my child," and "Mark my words, I will take what is mine." And here she sat, alone with Joanna in the cottage—the very place where the pirate had found her before.

Unable to shake her fear, she laid Joanna in the cradle and paced the cottage, the pirate's words echoing in her head. She checked again and again to ensure the shutters and the door were securely barred.

What if Hareford was hiding nearby, just waiting for her to open the door? They could not hide in here forever. They would need food, and soon her days of lying in would be over, and lessons with Philippe and William would resume. She would be vulnerable on the walk between the cottage and the manor house.

Joanna fussed. Thomasse picked her up and laid down, the babe nestled in the crook of her arm. Soon Joanna calmed and slept. Thomasse closed her eyes—and the dream came.

James stood in the doorway. She ran to greet him, Joanna in her arms. They shared a passionate kiss before James took the babe, lifting her high as she giggled.

Suddenly the cottage darkened. The pirate loomed in the doorway, sword drawn, fury etched on his face.

"I warned you." He pointed his sword at James. "Hand over the child."

Thomasse threw her body between them, but not quickly enough.

James lay bleeding on the floor, the pirate fleeing the cottage, the babe clutched in his arms.

Her eyes flew open, heart pounding so loud she could hear it. A cry tore from deep inside, and Joanna wailed in protest. Thomasse cooed and sang until the babe calmed.

How she wished James was here, holding her, soothing away her fears. But he was not—and somewhere out there the pirate roamed the isle—perhaps even now watching the cottage. The servant had called him desperate—and desperate men did reckless things. She would do what she must to keep them safe.

Why at such a time when she and James had grown closer? Sharing the cottage and caring for Joanna together had brought joy she had not thought possible. But now—his very presence could place them all in peril.

The door rattled.

She froze, not daring to breathe. With the door barred, whoever it was would not know for certain who was inside. That is unless Joanna cried.

"Thomasse, open the door."

James.

What was she to do? She had not had time to think it through. If the pirate lurked in the shadows, waiting for her to open the door, her dream could become real. She must send James away.

She rose from the mat and crossed to the door. Unbarring it, she opened it a crack. "Why did you come back?" Thomasse asked, her tone deliberately cold.

James stared at her, mouth agape.

"Joanna and I are well now. There is no need to continue coming to ease your conscience."

"I do not come out of guilt. You are my wife. Joanna is our daughter."

Thomasse placed a hand on her hip. "She is my daughter. Please—let me raise her in peace."

He blinked several times, then whispered, "Have you no heart?" His brow furrowed as he studied her face, the hurt plain in his eyes. "What a fool I have been to be so taken in." He turned on his heel and strode up the hillock.

Thomasse barred the door and dropped to the floor, tears flowing down her cheeks. She had not wanted to hurt him, but there was no other way to keep them all safe.

James turned and strode away. How wrong Madame had been about Thomasse. She had meant every word she said during her travail. What a fool he had been to believe she cared.

He should never have agreed to their marriage. The grief he had known when Becca and their babe died had nearly broken him, but it was fate that had stolen them away. Thomasse—she had made a deliberate choice to cause him pain. Now he was paying the penalty for offering his heart to someone who did not want it.

## Chapter Twenty-Seven

O ver the next week, Thomasse struggled with her fraught feelings: sorrow that James was probably gone from her life forever, and the need to convince herself it was for the best.

In time, James would realize she was not the same woman he had fallen in love with. Soon her lying-in would be over, and after her churching, he would want to claim his husbandly rights. He deserved better than a woman who would shrink at his touch—not because of any fault of his own, but because of the memories it stirred.

A loud knock on the door broke the silence, followed by "Thomasse, it is Madame de Beauvoir."

Thomasse unbarred and opened the door. Madame bustled into the cottage, her crisp white wimple contrasted with her sensible dark gray cotehardie. She placed her satchel atop the carved chest and leaned over the cradle to examine Joanna.

"Her cheeks are rosy, and she grows stronger every day," Madame said. "What of you, Thomasse? Any concerns?"

"My body has healed nicely," she replied, smoothing her loose-flowing kirtle. "We are both doing well."

Madame's gaze rested on her for a few moments. "Thanks to James. Without his attentiveness, neither of you would have survived."

Thomasse nodded. "Yes, I am grateful for that."

"I hoped you would use that time to finally begin building your lives together. Why did you send him away?" Madame asked.

"Does it matter?"

"Assuredly. It pains me deeply to see two people meant to be together torn asunder."

"Did James send you?"

"No, I came to check on your progress, though I am willing to render advice on matters of the heart."

"It is better this way. I am not the woman he fell in love with."

"And why does that matter? Over the course of a lifetime, we all grow and change."

"He deserves a woman who can be a proper wife." Thomasse chewed her lip. "He will find someone new soon enough."

"I suspect at one time you wished otherwise."

"That was before," Thomasse replied. "I am no longer ignorant. It lends a certain appeal to entering a convent."

"It is different, a beautiful thing, when two people love and trust one another."

"It is more than that. He and I come from two different worlds. I do not expect you to understand."

"First, I would say you are grasping for excuses. Second, I would say you are mistaken." Madame pulled out a chair from the table and lowered herself onto it. "Might I trouble you for something warm to drink?"

Too tired to argue, Thomasse retrieved two cups, ladled out the last of the warm broth from the kettle, and set them on the table.

Madame took a sip and set the cup aside. "I too am a daughter of the gentry."

Thomasse's eyes widened. "Indeed, I did not know."

"My family owns a manor a few miles south in St. Peter's Parish. They arranged a marriage, but I defied their wishes and married Geoffroi."

Recalling her father's vehement objection to her marrying James, Thomasse asked, "Did they cast you out?"

"They were furious at first. But when they witnessed our happiness, they softened. When William was born, they accepted my choice without reserve."

"Ah! That explains the bigger cottage." Thomasse wrapped her hands around the warm cup. "Did you ever regret your decision?"

"Not one day. The first years were hard, but our love carried us through."

"So it was worth giving up your privileged life?"

"In my humble opinion, yes. I had no desire to marry a man indifferent to me, to be treated as little more than chattel. Maybe some ladies care not, but I could not abide it. A noble title does not make a man honorable. Character does. It is not station that divides people, but rather pride and fear. In Geoffroi, I found a man I could love and respect, who made me complete. As the Bible says, the two shall become one. I only have this one life. I chose to live it on my terms."

"I am pleased things ended so well for you."

Madame placed her hand on Thomasse's arm. "And it can for you also, if you will just let it. I have seen the easiness between you and James, the great affection you have for each other."

"We are friends, nothing more."

"I refuse to accept that." Madame shook her head. "Tell me the real reason."

Thomasse looked away, not able to meet Madame's eyes. "The man who—" She hesitated, unwilling to say what had happened, grateful that she did not need to explain anything to Madame. "He does not want James near Joanna. He threatened to take her. If he finds us together, I fear he will kill James and take Joanna."

"Pray, do not take this amiss, but ofttimes, in our fear, our reason falters; it leads us astray, and we do things that lack sense. How are you and Joanna safer without James's protection? He has been right there beside you when you faced that man, ready to defend you, to fight for you."

Thomasse sipped on the broth as she contemplated Madame's words. "You speak truth. When it comes to the pirate and his misdeeds, my mind is troubled. James must surely think me a fool."

"My dear girl, you are not the first woman he has known who has suffered your fate. He understands that healing is no smooth road. When a man truly loves, as James does, he will be patient. That evil man has taken enough from you—do not let him take James as well."

Madame retrieved her satchel and headed to the door. "I ask you to reconsider. We all need someone who loves us, who can help soothe the torments of the soul. Go to him."

When Madame was gone, Thomasse knelt beside the chest James had made for her. She traced the delicate arches and flowers as she pondered the healer's words. Could she really find happiness being a wife? Madame had assured her she could.

She ran her finger along the outline of the heart-shaped lock. It was a thing of beauty. How many hours he must have spent crafting it, thinking of the joy it would bring to her. A token of his love. And she had not even thanked him.

Her vision blurred as she thought about the early days of their love. He had been so kind and generous, delighting her with little gifts of fruit and flowers. Before that horrible day, she had never treated him unkindly. But afterward, her words and actions had become unpredictable, often defying reason, even contrary to her own desires.

Joanna wailed, and Thomasse scooped up the babe and cuddled her close. She longed to feel James's arms around her, his soft voice telling her all would be well. With him, she always felt safe, just like that day on the cliff. His gentle care had given her a reason to live. But in her brokenness, she had driven away the best thing in her life.

A tear slipped down her cheek. She wanted to run to him, to plead for his forgiveness, to beg him to come home. But this time, she may have pushed him too far.

## Chapter Twenty-Eight

Thomasse entered the stable, her mouth dry, unsure if James would even speak to her after the way she had ordered him away from the bay-side cottage. She had thought to bring Joanna, for the babe might tug at his heartstrings, but it felt dishonest. If he returned, it must be for her alone.

Fortunately, Philippe came to visit and eagerly agreed to spend time with his goddaughter.

She found James cleaning the saddles, applying oil to keep the leather supple. He did not look up, but his shoulders tensed, making her suspect he was aware of her presence—and it was unwelcome.

"James," she whispered. "Can we talk?"

He poured more oil onto the cloth and resumed rubbing the saddle. "To what purpose? You made your wishes abundantly clear."

"Can you forgive me? I want you to come home."

Cloth still in hand, James turned about, dark circles shadowing his eyes. "I am not a servant you can summon or dismiss at will. You treat me as though I have no feelings. You have my ring on your finger, so you have no further need of me."

Thomasse stepped closer. "That is not true. You have been a true friend."

"You have a strange manner of showing it."

"I have done you wrong." She nudged at the rushes with her toe, unable to meet his gaze. "I love you, James."

"Words like *love* are easy to say when you desire something. But you can play a man for a fool only so many times. I married you because the seigneur commanded it—that is all."

151

"I do not believe you. The carved chest. A man does not spend hours creating something so beautiful for someone he does not hold in high regard."

James's eyes narrowed. "What does a daughter of the gentry know of love?"

"Very little, I confess. But I know when you are gone, I miss you. My heart longs to be with you. Whether good or ill happens, it is you I want to confide in. Are you saying you do not love me?"

"Maybe I felt that way once—"

"And now?" Her voice trembled. Could she dare to hope?

"I do not know what I feel." James swallowed hard and returned to oiling the saddle.

"I know I have wounded you. I never meant to, but sometimes fear takes over." She stepped up behind him and touched his arm, her voice soft and uncertain. "Can we find a way to mend this? If you will not do it for me, then for Joanna. She needs her father."

"I cannot." His words were strained, and he rubbed the saddle more vigorously. "It is wrong to expect me to live with you and not have you fully as my wife."

"I want that, too. I just need more time."

He turned and looked at her. "In other words, nothing has changed between us."

"It weighs heavy on my heart that I can never be the innocent girl who landed on Jersey. I do not want to let that pirate and what he did keep us apart." She looked down, unable to face him for fear the reminder would make him disdain her. "I cannot be with you as a pure bride. The day may come when you will resent me for it."

"Why would I hold that against you? You had no sway over that man's doings."

"Many men would."

"You are blameless—not just in my eyes, but in the eyes of God." He sagged against the wall, his voice weary. "What do you want from me, Thomasse?"

She stepped closer to him and placed a hand on his chest. His heart beat in time with her own. She breathed in his heady scent of musk, horses, oil, and hay. "Be patient with me. Help still my fear. When I turn from you, hold me close. Remind me it is my pain that speaks."

James placed his hand over hers. "You know I would never harm you, that my touch and my love are safe."

"My mind knows I can trust you, but my body still remembers and betrays me. I want to heal with you by my side."

His amber eyes stared deep into hers. "Are you certain?"

Thomasse looked up at him, her heart filled with joy at the tenderness in his eyes. She rose onto her toes and wrapped her arms around his neck. "I have never been more certain," she whispered against his mouth.

James gathered her close. When their lips met, she savored the taste of him. Her heart soared. This wonderful man—her husband—would be there for her today and always. The road ahead would not be easy, but they would walk it together.

*The End*

# *AUTHOR'S NOTE*

Unlike my other works, which feature historical figures, the main characters of Her Noble Groom are entirely fictional. Although their roles in this story are imagined, many of my secondary characters were real people—including the maiden in the green gown, her two charges, and the Bastard of Rozel. Even Magnar, the destrier, truly existed. Though his name is lost to history, this remarkable horse lives on in legend.

This novella is set during the first half of Book 1 of The de Carteret Chronicles: Legacy of Rebels series. Token of Betrayal delves deeper into Jersey's rich history, including:

- The story of the pirate, John Hareford

- The French Occupation

- The legend of the black horse

- And other fascinating events that occurred on the isle during the Wars of the Roses.

I hope you enjoyed Her Noble Groom. Please consider leaving a review. They help fellow readers discover great books. I'd truly appreciate yours at Goodreads, Amazon, or your favorite online book retailer.

Thank you.

# ABOUT THE AUTHOR

C.V. Lee writes about forgotten heroes and heroines of the past. She attended the University of Washington and majored in International Studies. This multi-disciplinary course of study helped her pull together the historical details necessary to craft the stories in The de Carteret Chronicles: Legacy of Rebels series.

Her fascination with Jersey history is personal. She learned about her family connection to the isle when her middle son was assigned a genealogy project in the second grade. Jersey was the home of her great-great grandparents. She found Jersey's history so compelling, she had to share the stories.

C.V. currently lives on an island in the Pacific Northwest. There she spends her days writing and enjoying her favorite hobbies: reading, cooking, travelling, and entertaining friends and family. She is a founding member of Paper Lantern Writers.

Learn more about C.V. Lee at:

- Her website, www.cvlee.com,

- On Facebook at C.V. Lee – Historical Fiction Author,

- Goodreads, or

- Follow on Instagram @cvleewriter.

# ACKNOWLEDGMENTS

Many thanks to Jenny Quinlan of Historical Editorial for her excellent developmental editing, and to my friends at Davis Writers Salon for critiquing my work each step of the way. Your thoughtful comments and constructive criticisms always elevate my writing to a higher level.

# ALSO BY C.V. LEE

### Novels
The de Carteret Chronicles: Legacy of Rebels series
Token of Betrayal – Book 1
Betrayal of Trust – Book 2

### Novellas
Her Noble Groom

### Anthologies
Unlocked – Joanna's Choice
Beneath a Midwinter Moon – Philippe's Epiphany
Destiny Comes Due – An Eye for an Eye

### Nonfiction
Crafting Stories from the Past: A How-To Guide for Writing Historical
Fiction
How to Research with Limited Source Material

www.ingramcontent.com/pod-product-compliance
Lightning Source LLC
Chambersburg PA
CBHW060224180626
46813CB00007B/2949